ONE THOUSAND WORDS FOR WAR

Edited by Madeline Smoot and Hope Erica Schultz

One Thousand Words for War
Edited by Madeline Smoot & Hope Erica Schultz

Children's Brains are Yummy Books
Dallas, Texas
www.cbaybooks.com

ISBN: 978-1-933767-51-2
eBook ISBN: 978-1-933767-52-9
Kindle ISBN: 978-1-933767-57-4
PDF ISBN: 978-1-933767-58-1

TABLE OF CONTENTS

INTRODUCTION

by Madeline Smoot and Hope Erica Schultz

Whether we like it or not, every day we are at war—with the elements, with our friends, with our parents, with Fate itself. Conflict permeates our day from the misunderstanding that leads to a fight with our best friend to the missed bus that makes us late for first period. We can't escape the conflict, the war, in our lives.

Or can we?

The authors in the nineteen stories in this book have set out to explore just that idea: Is conflict an inevitable part of the story of our lives? Does every story have to have conflict? And surprisingly, the answer is no.

The idea behind this anthology originated when we (Madeline and Hope) first discovered an online article on Kishōtenketsu, a traditional Chinese, Korean, and

Japanese narrative structure. To our surprise, these traditions had an entire story form that eschewed conflict in their plots. Having both grown up here in the United States, firmly rooted in the Western narrative tradition, such an idea was revolutionary to both of us. Could we create a science fiction and fantasy anthology that combined stories containing the conflict of Western tradition and stories inspired by the Kishōtenketsu form? We asked authors to submit their stories, and we have been awed by the response.

In this anthology you'll find conflict in expected places: a transgendered girl stands up to her bullies, a child soldier fights to keep his comrades alive, a group of teens wrestle with the elements to survive a time storm. At the same time though, you'll also find conflict missing in places where you would expect it to occur: aliens visit without the army becoming involved, a girl comes to terms with her friend's death. And finally, there are stories that combine elements of both, stories that combine the conflict of the Western tradition into the structured four part format of a Kishōtenketsu tale.

What all of the stories have in common, whether they contain conflict or dispense with it entirely, is their overall message of hope. Perhaps we are at war our entire life with time. Perhaps our day is filled with little battles. But even when we lose that battle, there is always hope for a better day. There is always the chance tomorrow for peace.

Madeline Smoot & Hope Erica Shultz

SHADOWLAND

by Valerie Hunter

Cavan walks carefully around the Pollaxes' property, the first time he's left the house alone. The sun is bright, which makes it easier, but he's still hesitant. He hates his lack of confidence, the strangeness of it all.

Though he has to admit it's pretty. He's at the edge of the Pollaxes' orchard, and the colors are brighter than in Zyss, the shadows softer. It smells prettier, sounds prettier, even feels prettier, as though beauty is a blanket wrapped around his skin.

It isn't home, though.

He sweeps this thought aside, squinting at the shadow ahead. A whirling purple shadow with what appears to be a sword.

It pauses mid-parry. "Aren't you the Pollaxes' foster? How do you move around so well?"

The voice is a little deep for a girl's, but melodious like some kind of horn. Cavan has been introduced to many people over the past four days, but he's sure he's never been introduced to this voice.

"Who are you?" he asks.

"Tirene. I live on the next estate. Answer my question."

Lady Pollax has bragged that the king's counsellor is their neighbor. If Tirene is his daughter, it explains why she knows about him. "I can see a little," he says, deciding not to mention how many times he's stumbled in the past few days. "What are you doing with that sword?"

"Practicing," she says like he's a dunce. "I'll be seventeen soon. They're letting girls into the Border Guard now, did you know?"

Father had spoken of it once, a diatribe about the downfall of the kingdom. "I heard," he says.

"I think I'll get in. I practice here every day."

"I'll leave you to it," he says, backing away.

"You can stay if you want." She goes back to parrying and thrusting. "There's a bench in front of you."

He only sees it because she mentions it. He hesitates, and then sits, watching her. She's fast. Her form is unconventional, too many unnecessary flourishes and swoops, but the more he watches, the more he realizes this will make her a formidable opponent. She's unpredictable, a lightning bolt with a sword. He gets caught up in watching her swooping shadow, pretending he's her opponent and planning his next move.

She pauses again mid-swing, and he can hear the scowl in her voice. "Who are you?"

A voice from behind Cavan says, "Begging your pardon. The Pollaxes' tutor, m'lady."

Cavan has met the Pollaxes' tutor, an older man with a reedy voice. The voice behind him now is deep and young. "You're not the tutor," he says, turning.

"I'm his son, Enver. I help tutor the daughters. You're the foster, aren't you?"

Cavan nods while Tirene says, "What are you doing here?"

"Just looking for a pleasant spot to read, m'lady."

"Never mind 'm'lady.' It's Tirene. What book is that?"

"A story about the Battle of Jullenna."

"Well, go on and read it," she says, flopping to the ground in a way Cavan finds amusing compared to her graceful swordsmanship.

"Aloud?" Enver asks.

"Read," Tirene commands, like she's the queen.

Enver has a pleasant voice, and it brings just the right excitement to the story. Cavan listens to the tale of a young soldier proving himself in battle, and he watches Tirene fidget in the grass as though she's fighting the battle herself.

When Enver finishes, Tirene springs up again. "You have any more stories like that?"

"The whole book is tales from the war."

"Read another," Tirene says and gets up, fighting the air again.

The next story is about a foster who chooses to fight alongside the son of his foster family. Cavan does not think he will ever want to do anything with the young Pollax boys, who spent their first meeting waving their fists toward his face in an attempt to see how blind he was while their mother silently attempted to stop them.

"I've never understood fostering," Enver says when the story ends. "I mean, I see the general idea—trading children to foster peace amongst the provinces—but it seems like there should be an easier way. One that doesn't involve sending your children to be raised by strangers. The Pollaxes' second son got fostered out at five!"

Cavan doesn't attempt to explain. How noble families are willing to sacrifice a son or two if it means an improvement in fortune, an alliance through marriage down the road, or simply a place to dump an unwanted child. Until recently, he hadn't understood it himself. In truth he still doesn't, though he knows all about it now. It's not something he wants to talk about.

So he says, "It's just the way of things," and leaves it at that.

They are a trio after that, gathering each day in the late afternoon at the edge of the orchard, Tirene with her sword, Enver with a book, Cavan just himself. Useless. Worthless.

Still, it's his favorite part of the day. Most of Enver's stories are about war and battles, and their predictability is soothing. The young soldier triumphs and is rewarded, or the old one fights his last battle bravely, sacrificing himself for comrades or kingdom.

One day, however, Enver reads a story of a young soldier who, faced with impossible odds and a terrible wound, quietly travels to another realm, one full of inhabitants who couldn't quite find their way in the kingdom. It is called the Shadowland, and Cavan perks his ears because isn't that where he lives, surrounded by shadows?

It ends with the young man uncertain whether he'll return to his kingdom now that he is healed. Tirene puts her sword down and complains, "I don't understand. Was he dead?"

"Maybe," Enver says.

Cavan thinks the Shadowland is not death but keeps his mouth shut, because who is he to say?

"It's too confusing," Tirene says.

Now Cavan speaks. "Every story can't be heroic sacrifices or miraculous wins. You know battle is probably nothing like the stories, right?"

"Maybe," Tirene says.

Enver laughs. "I know the difference between stories and reality, I just prefer the former."

So does Cavan, frankly, but he can't imagine a story that he will ever be the hero of.

When Enver speaks again, his tone is grave. "My whole life hasn't been books and stories. I've only been a tutor this past year."

"And before that?" Cavan finally asks, because Enver's pause is begging him to.

"I was training to be a healer at the Restorative Core. It was a great honor. My father arranged it."

"But it wasn't what you wanted?" Cavan asks. Tirene has gone back to fighting, but Cavan knows she's listening, the same way she always does when Enver tells a story.

"Oh, it was. Very much. I loved it at first. The learning. The knowledge that I would be someone who helped . . .."

This time Cavan lets the silence stretch. Enver will go on when he's ready.

"After two years is when they let you see . . . the Core's true nature. The basement cells, where they do their most noble work."

Cavan thinks he can see the word "noble" clawing through the shadows, red and prickly.

"They told us it was for the greater good. That we could find cures so others wouldn't suffer."

Cavan knows they take dead bodies to the Restorative Core. Noblemen are buried; everyone else is studied. Dissected. Disposed of. "The corpses upset you?"

Enver gives a rattling laugh. "No. The living bodies upset me."

"The . . . living?"

"They kept . . . afflicted people in the cells. All sorts. Fever addled, demented, crippled. They'd been assigned there, told there might be cures. There weren't cures. They were specimens. We prodded and cut and dosed, not to cure them but to satisfy our curiosity. Eventually, they died. Eventually, we killed them."

Enver's words are shadow arms threatening to choke him. Cavan can picture it: the dank cells, the afflicted being torn apart, begging for mercy.

"I left," Enver says, and he sounds like he's choking, too. "I couldn't . . . do that. The master healers and my father were angry. They said I showed such promise." He laughs that rattling laugh again. "What does that say about me, showing promise for that?"

"It doesn't say anything about you," Cavan says. "It says something about them."

"Maybe," says Enver doubtfully. "But anyhow, being a soldier can't be as bad as being an apprentice healer. If I kill as a soldier, leastwise it's a fair fight."

Cavan nods because he knows Enver needs him to.

Tirene has been fighting with the ferocity of a storm, and now she stops, pointing her sword at Enver. "You're always reading all those stories, but have you ever held a sword?"

Cavan knows that not acknowledging Enver's story is Tirene's way of being kind. He hopes Enver knows that, too.

"I've held a sword," Enver answers too quickly.

"Have you ever fought with a sword?"

Silence this time.

"Would you like to learn?" she asks with a little girl's excitement.

Enver goes to stand beside her. Cavan has never realized how tall Enver is, a rangy shadow of gangling limbs. Or maybe it's just that Tirene is small, though she never seems it. Even now, dwarfed by Enver, she doesn't seem it.

Tirene gives Enver a sword and stands behind him, positioning his hands and feet in a way that makes Cavan think of Father. He shuts his eyes against the memory, but that only makes it worse. He can always see more clearly with his eyes closed.

Father gave him his first toy sword when he was Aed's age, but he didn't teach him to use it until after the fever, until after the world was reduced to shadows.

Swordplay was all shadows. The most graceful of shadows. Father moved first for him, then with him in a way that was both comforting and clumsy.

He realized later that Father never really expected him to learn, not properly. Then one morning Father found him parrying with a sapling in the yard, and called, "Let me give you some real competition, son," in a voice that Cavan still clutched in his memory because there was such pride in it.

He was no longer an extension of Father after that. They moved from wooden swords to metal, the blades dulled so they wouldn't cause any real harm though there were bruises given on both sides.

Everyone who saw him fight marveled. He knew this was mostly due to his infirmity, but he also knew he had skill. Father said the cardinal rule of swordsmanship was caution, but Cavan disagreed. It was never worrying about anything but your next move.

He had limits, of course. He needed a clear day and an opponent in vibrant clothing. In an actual battle he'd be rubbish—too many distractions, too many competing shadows—so his skill had no practical purpose. He was just a nearly blind boy with a blunted sword.

But when he parried with Father, he didn't have to think about that. He could just fight.

He opens his eyes when Tirene starts complaining that Enver isn't moving correctly.

"I'm doing what you told me!" Enver protests, and Cavan agrees with them both. Enver is following Tirene's lead, but he looks all wrong.

"You're trying to make him move like you, but he's bigger than you," Cavan says. "You have to teach him to react his own way."

"What do you know?" Tirene says, though not unkindly.

Cavan gets up. "Give me your sword and watch," he tells Enver.

Enver obeys, but Tirene protests. "What are you doing?"

"Putting on a demonstration," he says, getting a feel for the sword and then checking that the tip is blunt enough not to hurt Tirene if he gets wild. Though he guesses Tirene can more than hold her own. "Shall we spar?"

"You're jesting!"

"I'm not half bad," he says, though he's not sure if that's true compared to her. He wants badly to find out. "And I think Enver needs to see how to defend, rather than be told."

The doubt rolls off Tirene in sickly yellow waves, but she raises her sword. "If you're certain."

"Certain," he says, touching his blade to hers, and then they're fighting. Or rather, he's fighting; Tirene is barely trying.

He knocks the sword out of her shadowy arm, and she splutters as Enver chuckles. "Full on, or don't bother," Cavan chides, and he can feel the air around her change, doubt and hesitation replaced by competitiveness.

They go at it. Tirene is still holding back a little, but so is he; they don't want to overwhelm Enver. Nevertheless, it's a battle, both of them exerting, flying about, the swords extensions of themselves.

All the afternoons of watching Tirene practice are what save him. She is talented and unpredictable, but he knows her, knows her flairs and feints as she makes them, can mirror them back and come up with a few of his own.

He's not sure how long they battle, a dance of limbs and metal, until Tirene catches him on the neck and he falls, the wind knocked out of him.

"I'm sorry!" Tirene says, a blur hovering above him.

His neck smarts but it's nothing compared to the joy of these past minutes. "I'm fine."

She helps him to his feet, and he grins as he gropes for his sword. "Again?" he asks her. "Or is it Enver's turn?"

"It is definitely not Enver's turn," Enver says. "Enver is full of awe for both of you, but no closer to actually understanding how to do that."

"Guess we'll have to slow down," Cavan says, still smiling.

Tirene hasn't raised her sword. "You're not actually blind, are you?"

Cavan laughs. "I can't tell you a thing about your appearance except that you're wearing red."

"Then how can you fight like that?"

"Instinct. Practice. Shadows. Shall we get on with our demonstration?"

They go through their moves at half speed, pausing to explain to Enver and answer his questions. The bruise on Cavan's neck pulses, and he enjoys how alive it makes him feel.

Eventually he gives Enver back the sword, and allows himself to feel a little pride when Enver manages to parry against Tirene. At the end of the lesson, Cavan and Tirene spar again, and he doesn't even care that he loses.

"I don't think I know you at all," Tirene says afterwards.

He doesn't think he knows himself, either, and it is a surprisingly nice feeling.

Cavan loses track of how long he's been in Solestair, as if the days themselves are shadows. He accompanies Enver to his classroom with the Pollax girls during the day and helps when he can, listening to and correcting the girls' recitations.

Late afternoons are for the orchard and Tirene. Enver is improving in his swordsmanship, and he and Tirene discuss the future in bright tones. Enver will receive his army assignment come spring, and Tirene is sure she'll be appointed to the Border Guard. Cavan will be seventeen by then as well, but he does not join in their conversations. He will not receive an army appointment no matter how many times he bests Enver in the orchard.

In truth Cavan has no idea where he'll be come spring. Fosterings are supposed to end at seventeen, when the boys are old enough to enter the army. Once upon a time he dreamed of the Zyssian command he would lead. Now the future is as shadowy as everything else in life, except these shadows are denser. Menacing.

He tries not to think of home, but it lurks every time he shuts his eyes. Are his sisters asking about him? Have the little boys forgotten him yet? Likely his parents don't mention him. He doesn't blame any of them, though: not Father for arranging his exile or Mam for allowing it. Not Aed, future Lord of Zyss, or the twins, whose arrival sealed his fate; they are Father's insurance should anything befall Aed.

He wished he hadn't eavesdropped. He can still hear their voices in his head, much as he wants to forget. Father telling Mam about Cavan's fostering. Mam protesting, saying it wasn't right, Cavan being their firstborn, and Father interrupting.

"Nothing's ever right, Marrin! It's not right he got the fever, not right he lost his sight. But it happened, and this must happen, too. How could he ever be Lord of Zyss? The lord has to be someone the whole province can trust above all else, be held equal to the king! Cavan couldn't even manage to judge a provincial fair let alone lead a regiment into battle."

Father's words haunt him now as he watches Tirene thrash Enver amidst both their laughter. They both have exciting futures, and he has a void.

Enver lays his sword down in defeat and calls to Cavan, "Give her some competition!"

So Cavan shuts away the future, picks up the sword, and has at it.

It's rare for Cavan to go to the orchard without Enver, but as a mild Solestair winter begins to hint at spring, Enver goes home for a few days to see his mam. It is the day before the army assignment letters, and Cavan reaches the orchard to find Tirene pacing.

"Did I ever tell you about my father's lists?" she asks, and her voice sounds as flighty as her body, as though it may burst. "His endless lists every spring? He made me think they were a game when I was small, let me pick . . .."

"Let you pick what?" Cavan asks. He has never heard this particular tone in Tirene's voice, and it scares him.

"The names!" she says, and something breaks in her voice. "The names of the boys who went to the Northern front. He would give me a list of names, and I would pick all the ugly sounding ones, and he would praise me."

Her anguish creeps into him, and he tries not to think of the horror of it. "Not your fault," he says.

"But I had a hand in it. He made me have a hand in it! I killed those boys."

"You didn't kill anyone," he insists, knowing she won't believe him.

"He's made his lists again. He doesn't ask me for help anymore, but I looked anyway." Her pacing becomes more frenzied. "Everyone thinks it's the king with all the power. And they don't mind, because no one questions a king. But really it's my father. The fosterings, the placements, the arrangements. They all go through him, because the king can't be bothered. We're all Father's puppets, and nobody even realizes."

"Does it matter if it's your father or the king?" he asks. "There's always someone in charge, and it's never us."

She whirls about. "How can you just accept that?"

"It's the way of things," he says, because it is.

"Enver's name is on the list for the Northern front." She hurls the words at him so they blot out the sun.

"Oh," he says, mouth gaping helplessly.

Her shadow rages around him. "You know he'll be proud to go. He'll think he's the hero of some story."

Cavan thinks Enver is not that simple, but he remembers Enver's eagerness to be a soldier because it will be a fair fight. Will his mind change with the odds against him? Likely not. Likely not at all.

"Couldn't you talk to your father?" he asks, not liking how small his voice sounds.

Tirene laughs a hysterical, humorless laugh. "My father doesn't listen to me anymore. Two years ago, I begged him not to send our stable boy to the Northern front. He made me deliver the letter with the king's seal myself. That's the kind of man my father is."

He tries to absorb the horror of this, tries to think of some kind of solution. He can't.

So he asks, "Did you make the Border Guard?"

"Yes." Her voice is dull.

"Congratulations."

"It doesn't matter now, does it?" she says.

He wants to tell her it does. It should. But he knows the words will be hollow, so he stays silent.

The next day he and Tirene wait for Enver. Cavan fingers the letter in his own pocket, thick parchment with the King's raised seal that Lady Pollax read for him this morning in the same sing-song voice her daughters use in lessons. Cavan's not sure whether Father is behind it, or what role Tirene's father may have played. Either way, it clearly wasn't part of the lists Tirene saw.

When Enver comes, his greeting reveals nothing. Tirene has to ask if he's received his letter.

"To the Northern front, yes," Enver says calmly, as though he's been invited to tea.

Tirene explodes. "You can't seriously be . . . accepting of this? Enver! Cavan, tell him."

He doesn't think he'll be much help, but he senses Tirene needs him to be. "Are you going?" he asks Enver.

"I've been ordered. What else can I do?"

"Not go!" Tirene yells.

"Do you want to go?" Cavan persists.

This time Enver pauses.

"Exactly!" Tirene snaps, jumping into the silence. "You know you don't want to."

"I don't particularly want to die," says Enver. "But someone has to survive, right?"

"No! You know no one survives the Northern front! The Alwaquims always defend their border ruthlessly, and they win! How many stories have you read about the Northern front! You know!"

"Yet the king keeps sending an army every year. He believes there's a chance we'll win." Enver's voice is insistent, pleading. Cavan knows he needs his stories, his hope.

"Don't be stupid," Tirene says ruthlessly.

When Enver finally speaks, his voice thick. "Going is the honorable thing."

"Forget honorable! Alive is better than honorable! Of

all the idiotic . . . ." She loses her words.

Cavan tries to find his. "She has a point."

"I know. I'm not stupid. I . . . what else can I do? Refuse, and be executed? I might as well die a hero." He pauses, and when he speaks again Cavan can hear the sad smile in his voice. "After all, my swordsmanship is improving."

"You're not even as good as Cavan, and he's blind!"

"Well," Enver says, like this is inconsequential. Maybe it is. Maybe all those stories really have turned his brain, or maybe it's just life itself, what happened at the Restorative Core and now this, telling him he doesn't deserve to live until he knows it in his bones.

You can't change a mind like that. Tirene can talk herself blue, but it won't be enough.

"I'll go with you," Cavan finds himself saying.

"What?" Enver asks.

"I'll go with you. If you run, or if you go to the Northern front. I'm coming, too."

"Cav . . .," Enver says, and Tirene is twirling again, an angry blur of red skirts.

"What?" Cavan says, gaining confidence. "If you can do it, so can I. I'll be an even bigger hero than you. Hardly anyone volunteers for the Northern front. Bet they write a poem about me."

"You are not helping!" Tirene says.

"They won't let you go," Enver insists.

"They will." He's not actually certain, but he isn't going to mention the parchment in his pocket. "I'm just as worthless as you."

Cavan goes to the orchard that night. He is surefooted even in the dark. Solestair still isn't home, though. He doesn't have a home.

He sits on the bench and isn't surprised when he hears Enver say his name.

"I don't know what to do," Enver says. He says it as a fact, not as a plea for help, so Cavan only fingers the parchment in his pocket.

"I've done bad things," Enver says. "At the Core. Maybe I deserve this."

"No."

"You don't know. There was . . . a girl. Fever blind like you. I . . .."

"You didn't know any better," Cavan says.

"I did! The first few times I didn't, it's true. I clung to the belief that I might help them, that it was worth the risk to try. But with her . . . I knew, but I was too scared to say anything against the masters. They had me remove one of her eyes, and . . . go poking around through the socket. The master told me I could try to remedy the problem, give her back the sight in her other eye. I knew I couldn't . . . I knew, but I persisted. Brought bits of her brain out while she shrieked gibberish . . . even if I had restored her vision, she wouldn't have been able to tell me . . . that was no cure . . . that was . . . ."

Enver sobs, and Cavan wants to vomit. He is that girl being tortured in the basement cell, not only sightless but voiceless as well.

He shoves the parchment at Enver, and Enver takes it, still crying. "What's this?"

Cavan has forgotten that it is dark, that at the moment Enver is blind, too. "My invitation to the Restorative Core."

Next to him Enver turns to stone, and Cavan tries to find the words to revive him. "Maybe you killed that girl, though I don't blame you for her death any more than I'll blame whoever the poor apprentice is for mine. Maybe you think dying in the North absolves you, but it doesn't. If you die, then I die, and the memory of that girl dies, and Tirene will be all alone.

"You want to redeem yourself? I'm your redemption. Forget about whether you want to save yourself. Save me."

He knows it will work. He knows Enver because he knows himself, knows how badly he wants to save Enver.

Finally Enver says, "I've been doing some research. Looking in books. I found a few mentions of a ship that appears in Mercolm Harbor the night before army reporting day and disappears by morning."

It isn't much, but it's something. "Where does it go?"

"I don't know, but it always comes back the next year."

"And the passengers?"

"I don't know," Enver repeats. "But I know how stories work. If the passengers were killed or tortured or sent somewhere horrible, we'd hear about it, to keep other people from running. There'd be some epic about the 'Coward's Way' or some such. But there's not. It's just a shadowy legend, some grand adventure."

"The Shadowland?" Cavan suggests, liking the idea.

"Maybe. Anyhow, it's better than getting annihilated by the Alwaquims or having a healing apprentice digging around your brain, eh?"

"Yes," he says, and he knows they have saved each other.

They don't talk much about the plan in the week that follows. They do tell Tirene, who asks, "What if the ship's not there?"

"I guess we'll swim," Enver says, but Cavan hears the strain behind his jocularity.

"What if it goes someplace awful?"

"Worse than the Northern front?" Enver retorts, and Tirene stops asking questions.

Cavan realizes in that week that time is watery. It flows and hitches and pours and sometimes he seems to be sinking in it, but it continues on steadily toward the night of their departure.

The day before, Cavan goes to the orchard earlier

than usual. Tirene is there with the swords, and they battle. Time turns into a steady rain, no end in sight, and he sees Tirene in the flashes of metal, the blur of purple, the dancing shadows. There are things he'd like to say to her, but he lets the sword do the talking.

When they are done—no winner, no loser, just a mutual winding down—she won't let him put the sword down. "Take it, in case you need it. I had it sharpened for you."

He puts a finger gently to the blade, frowning. "I could've hurt you."

She laughs. "I'm too quick for you."

"Thank you. For the sword. For . . .." He wants to thank her for many things, but he's not sure he can find the words.

"Don't," she says gruffly. "Just take care of yourself and Enver, all right?"

He nods. She dashes away before they can say goodbye, but maybe they already have.

He hefts the sword and fights the air, pretending he is Tirene. It makes him feel strong.

They leave in a heavy darkness, Cavan taking the lead because he is surefooted even as his heart trembles in his chest.

Eventually he's aware of someone following them, quiet but audible. He halts Enver with his hand, and they stand still in the blackness until a voice behind them says,

"Are we going to stand here all night or go to the harbor?"

"Tirene?" Cavan asks, more to inquire what she's doing here than to confirm her identity. There's no mistaking her voice.

"I can't let you have this adventure without me." Her voice is both light and urgent.

"What about the Border Guard?" Enver asks.

"They'll have to do without me. This sounds more exciting."

"We're doing this because we don't have a choice," Cavan says. "You—"

"Have choices? Do I?" She is quiet but angry. "I'll serve a year at most in the Border Guard, and then Father will arrange a marriage. Can you picture me a wife?"

He can't. He can only picture Tirene dancing with her sword.

Maybe he and Enver aren't the only ones who are doomed if they stay. Maybe they are not the only ones looking for redemption.

So they walk down the harbor road together, the darkness thick with promise, 'til Cavan can dimly see the harbor lights. "Is there a ship?"

"Yes," Enver says, squeezing his arm. "Small, but beautiful."

And he can see it then, too, an accumulation of shadows looming above the dock. His future. His redemption.

"Let's go," he says, and he knows it doesn't matter where the ship takes them, to the Shadowlands or elsewhere. They will be together, and it will be home.

Valerie Hunter is a high school English teacher and a graduate student at Vermont College of Fine Art's Writing for Children and Young Adults program. Her stories have appeared in magazines including *Cicada, Cricket,* and *Inaccurate Realities,* and in the YA anthologies *Cleavage, Real Girls Don't Rust,* and *Brave New Girls.*

BEFORE NIGHT FALL

By C. H. Spalding

Jared knew it was going to be a bad day when he saw that he had been partnered with Yousef.

Admittedly, up until the week before he would have been thrilled to be paired with the older boy; he'd had a crush on him since the second day of the summer internship near Elisium Three's arctic circle. Unfortunately, that crush had made him barely able to speak to Yousef, and when they'd finally actually talked with each other, it had been a very loud, very public argument about ethics in Terraforming. Yousef felt they were responsible for every animal they released and should do their best to ensure its survival; Jared had argued that a healthy ecosystem required them to step back and let nature take its course.

It might have been an interesting debate if they hadn't ended up yelling at each other.

Jared tapped his scanner to acknowledge the assignment and checked his gear. It was a typical tracking assignment, this time on a female arctic fox that had wandered out of her expected territory. The implanted chip would make the tracking easy enough, but they were still expected to treat this like a serious mission. A heat unit—in the unlikely event that they were out past sunset, a stunner—even though nothing dangerous to humans was in this sector, food, water, a medical kit, a pocket utility knife, and rope.

Yousef appeared to be going through the same check across the Rec Hall, and he waved cheerfully with no sign of ill feelings. Jared waved back self-consciously and checked his scanner again. The fox was twelve kilometers away; if they'd had any kind of transportation, it would have been trivial to get there. Transportation, unfortunately, was just one of the things missing out here on the Fringe.

"All set?" Yousef asked as he approached.

Jared looked up and swallowed. It was the eyes, he decided, that were so overwhelming—dark brown and huge under black brows.

"Ready," he managed and gestured to the door. He hit the chronometer function then set the alarm at the halfway point to sunset before striding outside.

The camp was in the middle of zone 12, an oasis of

Terraforming currently twenty kilometers across. Coming from the Center, it seemed barren. Instead of farmland, there was a carpet of moss and scraggly grasses. In the two weeks they'd been here, Jared had seen only a handful of birds and as many rodents. The highest predator in the zone was the arctic fox.

"It looks like Lucy has wandered out of the zone a bit," Yousef commented.

"You shouldn't—sorry," Jared stopped himself.

"Shouldn't name them," Yousef finished for him. "Numbers are less personal. But if we're to be stewards of this planet, I think it should be personal."

Jared shook his head and set out towards the blip on his scanner. "So this isn't just something to look good on your application to University. This is really what you want to do?"

Yousef matched his pace, smiling. "How many people get to shape a planet? I think I'd be bored by anything smaller, knowing that this was available. All of our grandparents were involved in this, and it's only through their success that people can do other things now."

The smile was just as dangerous as the eyes. Jared tried to divide his attention between his scanner and the terrain in front of them. "I'm not sure what I want to do yet," he confessed. "But I'm beginning to realize that I never appreciated travel by Tube or hot showers."

The walk went faster than Jared had expected; the cheerful catalog of things they both missed took up most of the two hours it took to get within thermal range of the animal. Jared switched over his scanner, and they both went silent as they looked. The area beyond the zone had patches of moss and grasses mixed with barren rock and sand.

"The chip's right there, but no thermal." Jared swore softly. "That's not good."

"I'll go thirty meters to the right, and we can triangulate," Yousef offered. He walked slowly, measuring his stride, and then turned back and started walking to the signal.

They both paused only a few feet from each other. The remains of the fox were just barely recognizable; some predator had left very little for them to find.

"There aren't supposed to be any larger predators in this zone," Jared protested.

Yousef crouched down beside the remains and took a sample, which he fed into his own scanner. "I've got this, see if you can find any tracks."

The hard ground left little enough behind, but a clump of moss showed a disturbing 5 toed paw print. Jared hurried back, his hand on his stunner. "It was a puma," he announced. "The closest zone with them is supposed to be zone 9. That's over a hundred kilometers away."

Yousef shook his head. "A big cat can travel farther than you think and shelter from Night Fall better than humans."

Jared snorted. "Nights beyond the Fringe would make forty below seem balmy. We should get back in and report this."

"I'm almost done." Yousef tapped his scanner a few times and then swore in two languages Jared knew and at least one he didn't. "She's been dead about six hours, and she was lactating. There are kits somewhere."

"Don't arctic foxes co-parent? Won't there be a father looking after them?"

Yousef shook his head. "There isn't a male missing. For whatever reason, she was on her own."

Jared checked his chronometer and swore. "Then we'd better start searching. We've got four hours to the half-way point."

Yousef raised an eyebrow. "I didn't expect you to agree to that."

Jared scowled impartially at the eyebrow, the situation, and himself. "If a puma killed this fox, then by definition this is not a stable ecosystem. If we're trying to build one, we need the building blocks to do that."

Yousef's mouth twitched, but he only nodded. "Spiral pattern?"

They set out in a clockwise spiral from the remains,

Jared watching the scanner for thermals while Yousef looked for signs of a burrow that could insulate the signature. It was slow, tedious work, and when the alarm sounded they were only two kilometers out from the dead fox, furthest from camp.

"We need," Jared began.

Yousef raised his hand. "We're only twelve kilometers from camp. The most we're going to get at this rate is fifteen. If we allow three hours to return, that will be plenty."

Jared grimaced. "That's not regulations." He looked at Yousef's patient expression and sighed. "Fine. I'll set it for three hours to sunset, and then we're out of here. No matter what."

Yousef grinned and slapped him lightly across the back. "No matter what," he agreed.

There was only half an hour left on the countdown when they found the cave. They'd found several dozen rodent holes and a few scrapes that could have been shallow dens, but this was more than large enough for a fox. Or a puma.

"Stunner in front, scanner in back," Yousef advised. "Got a preference?"

"I don't want to try to see around you," Jared lied. *I don't want to worry about you getting hurt.* He pulled out his stunner and started in. He was a few inches shorter than Yousef, but he had to crouch, and eventually to crawl. Yousef held a light with his free hand, and Jared's own shadow spilled in front of him, fragmenting his sight.

"Thermal in front of you, a little larger than I'd like," Yousef warned.

Jared took a deep breath and nodded, then moved forward. There was something moving in the darkness ahead, almost writhing, and his grip on the stunner tightened. He froze one long moment and then began to laugh.

"What is it?" Yousef peered around him, and then he laughed reluctantly, too.

A litter of eleven—no, twelve—baby foxes squirmed in the light. "This is going to be challenging," Jared said, shaking his head.

"I think the record is twenty-five in one litter, so we got off easy," Yousef offered. "But yes, once you have more than one per hand . . .."

The warning alarm went off while they were still arranging baby foxes, and Jared swore but kept fitting them into his jacket. They'd tied the bottoms as tightly as they could, and nestled the kits in, three to a side, six each. Yousef held the light between his teeth to free both hands.

"You take the stunner," Jared told Yousef. "There's no way I can get around you." He pulled out the scanner again, looking for any strays as they headed out. Yousef looked lumpy with the heat signatures of the babies under his coat. Jared opened his mouth to tease him; then his breath caught in his chest.

"Company, straight ahead."

Shooting around Yousef in the narrow passageway while crawling with six fox kits in his jacket was impossible, but he still transferred the scanner to his left hand and pulled his own stunner. There was a flash of eyes in the darkness, then a growl that climbed to a shriek in front of him, followed by the blue pulse of Yousef's stunner.

Yousef spat out the light with a curse. "Well, the good news is that it's unconscious. The bad news is that it weighs a fair bit more than me, and I can't squeeze by it."

Jared clenched his hands to keep from looking at his chronometer. "Why don't you hand back the fox kits, so you can push without worrying about hurting them?"

It was more time wasted, but there was no sense in commenting on it. Jared shoved each of the kits into his own jacket. It felt like wearing a vest of living, scratching flesh, but it distracted him from not being able to help with the puma.

Yousef shoved the animal forward, inch by inch, and Jared kept up a steady stream of cheerful encouragement. "That's it. All part of the glamorous job of sculpting a planet, now with bonus exercise session."

Yousef at last was able to scramble past the big cat and Jared hurried after him.

"I can take," Yousef began.

Jared cut him off. "No time. Start running." Yousef

glanced at the puma, and Jared shook his head. "Don't even think about it. He'll wake up in time, or he won't."

The sun was lower than he'd hoped, but there was no sense in checking the chronometer now. Jared started running, arms around the jacket to cushion the kits. Yousef ran beside him, and they kept going, racing the light.

The temperature began to fall, the air crisp in Jared's lungs as he took each breath. Shadows lengthened. They had five kilometers to go just to get back into the zone, where survival was theoretically possible at full dark, then another ten to the safety of camp.

The moss and grasses had formed a complete carpet again by the time the light was too low for running. Yousef switched back on his light, the stunner still in his right hand. "I should have agreed to head back at the half way point. I'm sorry."

Jared choked a laugh. "And missed all this fun? Don't be silly. Have you turned your heater on yet?"

Yousef shook his head in the twilight. "It only lasts six hours."

"If we're not back to camp in six hours, I think we can safely say that we're dead. Turn it on." Frost was forming on the grasses below their feet, and a breath through his nose gave Jared the sensation that all the hair inside had frozen stiffly at attention. He clicked on his own heater and pulled down the mask from the jacket's hood. "We're going to need the scanner to home in on the camp."

Yousef holstered the stunner and pulled out the scanner, adjusting their course minutely. "I'm sorry about last week. About yelling at you."

"Yeah, well, I yelled back." The rush from the heater barely kept up with the cold seeping into him. Jared stomped his feet a little as he walked, worked his fingers in his gloves. He couldn't really feel either any more. "Not to resume the fight or anything, but I think the answer is probably somewhere in between." He cleared his throat. "So, I was wondering if you'd be interested in giving me some advice. There's this guy back at camp that I'm interested in, but I'm reluctant to say anything because it could get awkward with us all stuck here for the summer."

Yousef laughed. "We're going to spend our trek for our very survival talking about your love life?"

"Well, yeah, I figure it beats talking about our funerals, and it's only a little scarier." Jared laughed at himself. Now that he was walking, the kits were settling down, hopefully sleeping. "So, what do you think?"

Yousef walked in silence for a few moments. "Ask him if he wants to get coffee. He'll likely know where you're going, but he can say yes or no without making it a big deal. Then you can see where it goes."

"Ah. Brilliant. I think I'll do that." Jared walked on. He

was starting to feel warm again, and from everything he knew, that was a bad sign. "What do you plan to name Lucy's babies?"

Yousef took his arm when he started to stumble, but they continued debating names. After they'd settled on twelve girl names and twelve boy names—since they hadn't had time to check the kits for gender—Jared fell to his knees mid sentence.

"I'm just going to take a break. It's nice and warm here."

Yousef whapped him up side the head. "Hey, none of that. The camp is right over that rise, and then you get to ask somebody to have a cup of coffee. No putting that off for a nap."

Jared squinted up at him. "No?"

"No." Yousef hauled him back to his feet. "Just over that rise. I promise."

They trudged together, step by step. They stepped over the rise into the circle of a search light, and Jared sighed.

"You had no clue that the camp was actually here, did you?"

"None whatsoever," Yousef agreed.

They stumbled forward towards the camp's perimeter, where anxious researchers and interns converged on them. As they were pulled towards the medical building, Jared looked up and met Yousef's eyes. "Hey, after the whole frostbite and taking care of the babies part . . . you want to get a cup of coffee?"

Yousef raised the perilous eyebrow again and smiled the dangerous smile. "Yes."

C.H. Spalding has been writing short stories since the 1980s or before. Only claim to fame: having dinner with Anne McCaffrey in 1992, then nervously pushing her in a wheelchair around the Atlanta airport to get her to her flight. She wanted to take the escalator at one point. Oh God, the terror.

UNEXPECTED GUESTS

By Laura Ring

Hina, make the tea. Quick!"

Sindhis are the most hospitable people in the world. Or so my mother says. And if you look at our village, or any other fishing village on the outskirts of Karachi, you'll see the truth of it. Our houses are made of jute and twine—flimsy, ramshackle things. Our roads are unpaved. The well where we fetch water is a fifteen minute walk away.

But our *mehman-khana*? The place where we receive our guests? Where we welcome strangers and far-flung loved ones alike? It is beautiful. Solid, baked brick, whitewashed, with an inlaid pattern of stars and diamonds painted deep blue and soft green.

I've spent many hours with my female cousins scrubbing salt crystals off its walls, brushing sand off the floor with a long-bristled *jharoo*. There are years when the summer storms off the Arabian Sea are so strong, that the guest hall is the only structure left standing. Everything else must be rebuilt.

For years, I've stood outside the hall looking in while relatives from other villages bring offers of marriage for my older cousins. I've just turned fifteen; it won't be long before those offers begin to come for me.

Once we hosted a foreign lady from the city, who took hundreds of photographs of the children and the broken boats on the shore. We even had a politician from Malir, who asked our men all kinds of questions about water and electricity and "basic services."

But today's guests were truly unexpected.

No one was sure how they got here. Our village is miles from the nearest town, but there was no sign of a car or bus or donkey cart. They were dressed in black *burkas*, all three of them. You couldn't see an inch of skin at their feet or wrists, and they kept their eyes fixed at the ground. Thankfully, all our men were out fishing. My mother swept them into the guest hall and sent me for refreshments.

I made tea in a large pot over the open fire, half water, half buffalo milk, the cream mixed in. Lip-scalding hot.

Plenty of sugar. I defy you to find a better cup of tea in all of Pakistan.

I poured the tea into four glass cups (our guests should not have to drink alone!) and bore them, along with fresh water, on a tray to the guest hall.

I took my seat on the floor next to my mother, who was introducing the women of the village. "And this is my daughter, Hina," she said. I smiled and bowed my head shyly.

Our guests did not speak. I lifted the tray in offering, and the three strangers reached out and took the cups in their hands. Their modesty was extreme; again, not even a hint of flesh was revealed. I offered the final cup to my mother and sat back to watch them drink.

Something magical happens when strangers become guests. That was doubly true here.

At the first sip, all three sets of eyes flew instantly upward, meeting my mother's and mine. I'm certain my heart stopped, for their eyes were huge, oblong and pupil-less orbs, their skin pale green and hairless.

Our three guests rose as one, no longer averting their gaze. They bowed and nodded, acknowledging each woman seated in the hall. As we followed them outside, I noticed that they left no marks in the sand; they seemed to float several inches above the ground.

"God keep you," my mother said.

How can I describe the strange craft that hovered in the sky above us? We had no words for it. We stood motionless while the three guests rose, pulled by some unseen force, and sifted into the ship. Within seconds, they were gone.

Through some silent agreement, none of us ever spoke of this day again—the day we welcomed the star-farers as our honored guests. I cannot help but wonder why they chose us—and why they chose to reveal themselves to us—years before the official "first contact," before galactic treaties and interplanetary migration made the star-farers our neighbors and our friends.

Perhaps my mother is right—that the fame of Sindhi hospitality knows no boundaries. As for me, I hope it is not prideful to hold onto the memory of those three glass cups, each drained dry.

We really do make extraordinarily good tea.

Laura Ring is an anthropologist and academic librarian living in Chicago. She is the author of *Zenana: Everyday Peace in a Karachi Apartment Building* (Indiana University Press 2006).

THE COMMANDER

Steve DuBois

It was all in pieces. The bits of Fabrice's weapon were arrayed before him, cleaned and oiled and ready for assembly, each component glinting dully under the tropical sun. But his stomach was growling with hunger, and the buzzing of the flies on the riverbank matched the buzzing in his head, and as he stared down at the pieces, he could not for the life of him remember how to put them back together again.

He had been taught how to perform the task. The months—years, now?—under Sergeant Muteba's leadership had taught Fabrice, and the other boys, a great deal. How to assemble and disassemble a weapon. How to scrounge for food in the unlikeliest places, and when necessary, how to make a meal of grubs and grass. The boys had been taught how to hold their nerve when the

air filled with screams and hot metal, and when the enemy charged them across the broken fields, bayonets fixed
and eyes wild with bloodlust. How to swallow their fear
and raise their rifles and squeeze the trigger, not pull it
but *squeeze* it, yes, just so; and how to watch the light go
out in the enemy's eyes. And how to think that this was a
good thing, yes, a thing well done. They had been taught
how to hold to the line next to one another. And on those
occasions when the line collapsed, they had been taught
how to bury one another. And how also to bury that other
life they'd lived, in those now-extinct towns and villages,
so long ago. Yes, that above all. The boys had been taught
to forget. And now, sure enough, Fabrice had forgotten.

"Your weapon is your life," Muteba had shouted at the
boys, morning after morning, and here was Fabrice's life,
in pieces before him. There was the spring, the bolt, the
bolt carrier. There was the receiver, the dust cover, the
gas tube. He had taken them apart and put them together
a hundred times, but his head spun and today he could
not make them fit. Last night's supper had been only a
handful of cassava, and he had given his portion away to
Sony, who had been so exhausted after the twenty-kilo
hike into the highlands that it had looked like he might
never again be able to stand. Perhaps it had done some
good, for Sony had risen again the next morning and had
joined the column. Sony was several boys down the line

from him now, sitting cross-legged on the riverbank, re-assembling his own weapon. Muteba was coming back up the ranks, fixing each boy in turn in his yellow-eyed glare, and it seemed to Fabrice that Sony was doing well, considering. But Fabrice's own head spun with hunger, and he could not make the pieces fit.

He will beat me, Fabrice thought, *and I am in no shape to take another beating. He will kill me, and there will be no one left to shield the other boys from him. Eshele, who loves books . . . Malaba, who talks of nothing but girls . . . Gaussou, who plays the consummate soldier and shouts his love for war, but who is kind enough when he thinks no one is watching. Even Kama, with his red eyes and white skin, who is the most obvious target in every engagement but who never, ever gets shot, who says he cannot die, because he is a ghost already. They will put me in the ground, and they will move on, but there will be no one to protect them from Muteba.*

Fabrice fumbled with the spring, his hands shaking, and sought to thread it clumsily around the bolt. And that was when he heard the voice.

"No, boy!" it said. "This is not how it is done."

Fabrice looked up. The voice had been that of a full-grown man, rich and booming, full of weight and purpose. It was the voice of one who, unlike Muteba, felt no need to shout. Yet when Fabrice looked up, there was no man present. Only the boys, cross-legged on the ground, and Muteba, more beast than man, working his way up the line.

"Look at the all pieces before you," said the voice, not unkindly. Fabrice looked down, and all the parts were there. "It is a complex task, for one as young as you. A monumental task, even. Like eating an elephant." There was a loud smack and a cry from down the line; Muteba was disciplining one of the smaller boys for some trivial fault. "Tell me, Fabrice, how does one eat an elephant?"

Fabrice looked up again. There was no man there. The other boys were playing a cruel joke on him, but who among them could pull it off? Who had such a voice? "I . . .," he began. "I don't . . .."

"One bite at a time," said the voice. "One eats an elephant one bite at a time. Here. Allow me to assist you."

Fabrice looked down. There was no act of will on his part; instead, he saw his hands go to work of their own accord. There was none of his boyish clumsiness in them; they did not shake with hunger or fumble with the gun's components. Every action was strong, sure, and entirely outside of his control. The small end of the bolt slid into the bolt carrier, rotating counter-clockwise to seal with a click. The end of the bolt carrier group then matched up with the hole in the gas piston chamber, notches and openings aligning. As he watched, his hand pushed the carrier down and slid it into place. Next, the spring slid into the rear opening of the bolt carrier group . . . and Fabrice was suddenly reminded of an evening in Muteba's tent, the Sergeant drunk on lotoko mash and calling out to him, beckoning him closer, his face leering, his voice full of false cheer, his belt undone. Fabrice struggled to forget what had followed, but all the while, his hands never paused in their task. The rear end of the spring was already aligned with the notch in the receiver, and his hands had folded the rear sight forward; the front end of the dust cover was in place, and as his hands pressed down it shut with a snap.

"One bite at a time," the voice repeated, and the strength and surety faded from Fabrice's hands; they were once again his own, the hands of a boy, not of a man. Muteba was before him now, staring down yellow-eyed at Fabrice's reassembled weapon. Fabrice stared steadily at the ground. *I will not countenance eye contact*, Muteba *says. Do not look up at him. You know what will follow if you do.*

At length, out of the corner of his eye, Fabrice saw the older man nod sternly, then proceed to the next boy.

Muteba had told them, many times, not to look directly at him. He had also told them not to talk. *I will not countenance discussion in my presence,* Muteba said. *"When you are alone with one another, you may be boys.*

But in my presence, I countenance only soldiers." So why am I not being punished? Did Muteba not hear the voice?

"Of course he cannot hear me," said the voice, as if in answer. "Nor can the other boys. Only you can hear me, Fabrice. For it is you whom I have chosen."

"Who. . .who are you?" Fabrice whispered. "Are you a demon? And for what have I been chosen? Will you steal my soul?"

There was a brief silence. "No, Fabrice," said the voice. "I am not a demon. Though some might say I once was one. And though your soul is of interest to me, I am not here to attain it for my own purposes.

"Who am I? I once had a name, though I scarce remember it. But you and the other boys are soldiers, no? A soldier has no name. A soldier has only a rank. Therefore," the voice concluded, "let us call me the Commander."

It was another engagement. There were no battles in Sergeant Muteba's world, only "engagements." Battles were things to be feared. Sergeant Muteba did not countenance fear. Battles were said to be glorious, and these things that happened to them every few days were not glorious in the least. So, yes. Engagements, not battles. Just so.

The routine was well-established. They hunted and tracked the rebels through the bush, or the rebels hunted and tracked them. Sooner or later, they came upon one another, and there followed a sputtering, flickering mess, devoid of tactics or strategy. The boys and their enemies dove behind logs or into ditches; they took turns spraying bullets randomly into the opposite foliage in the hope that someone would pop their head up at the wrong time. Muteba, leading as always from the rear, would scream at them to advance; occasionally, one of the new boys would heed him and, invariably, would be scythed down. The long-term survivors, such as Fabrice, knew that to obey the order was to die, but to ignore it and pretend not to have heard was acceptable. The Sergeant could not live with the shame of being disobeyed, so if everyone disobeyed, he had to pretend never to have given the order at all. Eventually one side or the other would grow tired of the fiasco and retreat. Then it would be time to bury the bodies—men, occasionally, but usually the corpses on the other end of the fight were those of boys no older than themselves. The men of the nation had long since been used up. And then would come night, and Muteba would cook up the lotoko mash, and whatever boy had fought best in Muteba's eyes would be "invited" to share it and to share the Sergeant's tent as well.

It was better not to fight too well. Better to keep your head down. And best of all, perhaps, would have been not to fight at all. But that was not an option, and with Muteba at the rear, any boy who fled would be shot down by the sergeant's own weapon.

They fought the rebels over anything or over nothing. Today they were fighting over a forest clearing. The rebels were hunkered down in the opposite trees, which extended rightwards up a gentle slope to a low bluff that commanded the whole battlefield. Fabrice and his comrades were ensconced behind a low rise in the tall grass on the other end of the clearing. It was gradually becoming obvious, however, that there was something different about today's enemies; there was a pattern in the bursts from their guns, evidence of a plan, of sorts. Fabrice would have scented the danger even if the voice of the Commander had not suddenly emerged from nowhere. "Fabrice," it told him, "they are trying to outflank you."

Fabrice snuck a quick glance over the rise. It was true; there had been distinct movement in the trees off to the center-right. The enemy was seeking to gain a position on the bluff; if they gained it, they could pour enfilade fire into Muteba's boys, attacking both from the side and from an angle above, rendering their cover useless. Fabrice and his companions would be massacred.

Muteba was, as always, screaming at them to advance. *That would be even more suicidal than usual,* Fabrice thought. *Advancing a flanked position will leave us entirely surrounded.*

"What can I do?" Fabrice whispered. "I cannot retreat.

I cannot advance, and I cannot stay where I am."

"Think, boy!" The sonorous tones of the Commander's voice were somehow clearly audible even over the pop and crackle of the rifle fire. "They seek the bluff. Their attention will be directed at your current position. Prepare properly, and you may pay them back in their own coin."

Fabrice swallowed and nodded. The next bit would be the hardest part, but if he could carry it off, he would save the whole platoon. *That is, if I can survive Muteba . . ..*

Fabrice desperately crawled backwards behind the rise. Then, protected from the enemy by the sloping ground in front of him, he popped up into a crouch and raced off to the right at a dead sprint. He heard the Sergeant shouting behind him, heard the hum of bullets close behind as Muteba fired at him, but he managed to dodge and roll into a hollow beside Sony and Pierre, one of the new boys. Pierre's eyes were wide, his rifle preposterously huge in his tiny hands. He had been the youngest boy taken on the latest "recruiting drive," and was in truth too young even for this battalion. It had taken all of Fabrice's persuasive powers to persuade Muteba to take him on as a soldier rather than to throw him into the burning hut beside his parents.

Quickly, Fabrice explained his plan. He would require covering fire in two directions—one boy would have to hold off the enemy, one would have to hold off their own sergeant. They nodded agreement, and then Fabrice was off again, like a shot, into the trees to the right, the gunfire chattering away behind him.

Slow and silent, Fabrice worked his way deep into the woods, then circled back left. By the time he arrived at the clearing, the bluff now directly in front of him, three of the enemy had already gained command of its heights. They were preparing to fire down upon Fabrice's comrades. But it was as the Commander had foreseen. They were used to fighting pigheaded, straight-ahead types like Muteba. It had never occurred to them to think that someone might see them coming and prepare a surprise of his own.

Fabrice raised his weapon to his shoulder. The first shot took one of the enemy, a full-grown man with the look of hard-won experience, cleanly in the back of the head. The second, a man with skin so black it was almost purple in the afternoon light, turned just in time to catch the remainder of the burst full in the chest.

The third man was no man at all, just a boy, no older than Fabrice himself, his skin sallow and pitted with acne. His eyes were wide with terror, his weapon lowered; he knew he was done for. Fabrice raised his rifle again . . .

. . . and suddenly, for the second time, Fabrice's hands were not his own. He had intended to put a shot cleanly through the boy's forehead, but instead, his burst went skyward. The boy before him screamed, dropped his rifle, and ran, disappearing down the bluff and into the trees beyond.

Fabrice was livid. "Why?" he growled in a hoarse whisper. "They were the enemy! They wanted to kill us! They deserved to die!"

The Commander's voice was laden with regret. "Fabrice," it intoned, "the first two deaths were necessary, to save your friends, but they were not deserved. No one in this war, save those who perpetrate and profit by it, deserves to die. And the third boy . . . his death was neither deserved nor necessary."

Fabrice scowled and kicked a stone into the underbrush.

"I fear, Fabrice, that you have seen too much death. I fear that you have grown too used to it, that you have grown a callus on your soul. Yet I have also seen you show mercy and wisdom. You, of all these boys, are the only one who can . . ."

The voice cut short as, suddenly, Muteba came racing out of the undergrowth and onto the bluff, followed by most of the other boys. "COWARD!" he roared. "TRAITOR! YOU HAVE DENIED US . . .." He suddenly stopped short, staring like a stupid ox at the two corpses on the hilltop, and at the still-smoking barrel of Fabrice's rifle. And slowly, very slowly, a smile spread across his face as he realized exactly how close he had come to disaster and exactly how that disaster had been prevented.

"Ah!" He shouted with sudden discovery. And then again, "Ah! A cunning stratagem, to be sure! An advance against the enemy, just as I ordered!" Muteba raised a warning finger to the other boys, who cast down their eyes before his withering glare. "Did I not order you? And here, finally, is a soldier who takes orders!" He suddenly surged towards Fabrice and ensnared him in a monstrous bear hug, laughing wildly. Fabrice fixed his own eyes on the center of the big man's chest, smothered under his attentions. "I am a commander who will always countenance cunning and bravery! And Fabrice is cunning and brave, indeed!"

With one of the sergeant's arms still around him, Fabrice was whirled around to face the rest of the company. "A cheer for Fabrice!" The other boys raised their rifles in a ragged cheer, but Fabrice never saw them. His eyes were fixed on two figures in the distance, their backs turned, dragging two corpses towards the assembled battalion. Even from afar, Fabrice could recognize the bodies—Sony and Pierre, each riddled with bullets. Perhaps the bullets of the enemy, perhaps the bullets of Muteba and their comrades; who could say? And from a glance at the eyes of the boys around him, Fabrice knew that they would not say what role they might have played in the deaths of the two boys who had watched his back. They were already forgetting.

We have all become so good at forgetting.

The entrenching tools were already out, digging a pair of shallow ditches, but Fabrice was being half-dragged back to camp, Muteba's arm tight around his shoulders. "This calls for a celebration, don't you think? Yes, certainly! Let's have a drink, you and I, my brave boy . . .."

Night had fallen. The firelight glistened off of Muteba's bare, brawny, scarred torso. Fabrice sat before him, eyes averted, as the sergeant scooped up yet another cup of lotoko from the basin. There were cobs floating in it, which meant that this would be a blind-drunk; tomorrow, the sergeant would barely be able to see. Fabrice could empathize. He had his own worries about seeing tomorrow.

"Command is a lonely burden, my boy, and a heavy one." He offered the cup to Fabrice, who shook his head, his eyes downcast. The big man shrugged and raised it to his own lips for a long gulp, then continued. "No man who has not picked up the burden can know its weight. No man can know the pain I feel at the loss of each soldier under my protection. Did you know that, Fabrice? Did you know that I feel these losses? You can look at me, you know. You have earned the privilege. I will countenance eye contact, under these unique circumstances."

Fabrice kept his eyes low, and his face expressionless.

Muteba responded with another shrug. "As you will. It is true, though. I feel each loss." He shook his head. "But it is not the luxury of the commander to allow himself to feel these deaths as keenly as he might. For if the commander succumbs to grief, who will lead his soldiers? Who will ensure their safety and the success of the mission? No. To be a commander is to learn to put one's own deepest feelings aside. It is but one of the many sacrifices one must make. One cannot look back. One must advance, my boy. One must always advance."

"Now, you, Fabrice," spoke Muteba, gesturing sloppily at him with the crude wooden cup, "it seems to me that you have the stuff of command in you."

A voice spoke, rich and resonant, a voice only Fabrice could hear. "Indeed."

"But you care too deeply, Fabrice," Muteba said, his words slurring. He shook his head again. "The boys will follow you. You proved that today, with Sony and the other one. They would risk their lives for you. But to allow yourself to care as you do? That is a mistake. To care too much can drive a commander mad."

The voice spoke again. "And you have no idea, fool, just how mad the Commander has become."

Fabrice risked a glance up. Muteba's eyes were already clouded with drink, his reactions slow and unsure, as he reached out an arm, wrapping it around Fabrice's shoulders.

"Let me help you, Fabrice," he said. "Let me show you, as one soldier to another, how to cope. I will teach you to go away to a place inside where you cannot be hurt, where one can do that which needs doing without shame. Let us give you some practice." And Muteba's voice hardened for a moment as he reached down to loosen his belt. "That is an order, and I will not countenance dissent."

The voice spoke a third time. "No more than we shall countenance you any longer, Muteba." And when Muteba looked down at Fabrice, he saw a nine millimeter pistol in Fabrice's right hand, pointed directly at his heart. And when Muteba looked at his own belt, he saw his sidearm holster unlatched and empty.

"Your weapon is your life," Fabrice whispered. Muteba's eyes widened for a moment, and then a strange smile creased his face as he understood.

And the voice of the Commander spoke. "Here is a death, Fabrice, which is both deserved and necessary."

Muteba grinned at Fabrice. "Ah. But are you sure, boy? Have you truly learned the lessons I have tried to teach you? Are you truly ready to be a leader?" And Fabrice found that even now, he could not look Muteba in the eye. And he knew that, in truth, he was not ready.

But he knew one who was.

"Allow me to assist you," spoke the voice. And Fabrice's hands were not his own, and they did not pull the trigger, no, but *squeezed* it, yes, just so, just as Muteba had taught him. There were two shots, surgical in their precision. And when the other boys came running to Muteba's tent, their rifles at the ready, they found Muteba flat on his back, bleeding out in the dirt, and Fabrice standing over him, the pistol in his hand.

The boys stood in a half-circle, surveying the scene. At length, it was Kama who spoke. "This is not a bad thing you have done, Fabrice. But it will end badly for us. Now it will not just be the rebels who want to kill us, but the government as well. Now there is nowhere for us to run or hide. Now there is no one to lead us and tell us what to do. You have saved us, but you have doomed us as well."

Fabrice opened his mouth to agree, but his voice was not his own. Though Fabrice's voice was that of a boy, it suddenly held the authority of a man. "You are mistaken, Kama," he heard himself say. "I have led you into peril, but I will lead you out again. Now you must trust my authority, and obey my orders. For I am the Commander."

The journey was long and brutal, upriver and across the highlands and down again into the swampy, verdant, mosquito-infested plains. Kama had not been wrong in his prediction. The sporadic bands of rebels were only half the trouble. At some point the government forces must have worked out what had happened, because the boys were pursued. They travelled for fourteen hours a day, then for eighteen, then for twenty. It seemed to Fabrice that he barely shut his eyes at night before the Commander's voice woke him, and he was shaking the other boys out of their own slumber and piling them back into the column and onwards.

All along the way there was conflict. And all along the way, there was mystery—for Fabrice had suddenly become a master of trickery and deceit, doubling back across streams to confound the enemy's dogs, directing the boys to lay snares and rig deadfalls and dig pits to catch their pursuers. Had Muteba once taught them tricks like this? It seemed to some of the boys that he had, but who could remember? What had become of Fabrice? What could explain his transformation?

As for Fabrice, he could no longer converse as one boy to another with his former friends. Now, when they looked upon him, their eyes held not gratitude, but awe. Muteba had not been wrong; command was a heavy burden. But Fabrice refused to allow his duties to harden his heart. Whatever he allowed the Commander to do with his hands or with his voice, his heart remained his own.

And finally, one day, they crossed the great western river, on the far bank of which lay another nation. And there the tents with the red cross beckoned, and the men and women in the sky blue helmets waited with all the food a boy could eat and all the rest a boy could desire. With a chance at a new life, and with a chance to forget.

But Fabrice was not allowed to forget because the Commander would not grant him the gift. Instead, the Commander made him remember.

Fabrice struggled to dam the tide, but the Commander's influence was inexorable. It all came rushing back in upon him—the months of horror and pain, the harsh days and the harsher nights, all of Muteba's cruelties, all of his fallen friends. All of the unspeakable "recruiting drives," all of the things he'd been made to do to strangers in order to fill the holes in the platoon. And back further still, to the day he himself had been made a soldier—to the mother and father who'd loved him, and to what had been done to them before his eyes. And Fabrice had thought the pain would crush him utterly. He had curled up into a ball and had cried inconsolably for hours on end. It was a week before he emerged from his cocoon of pain, and when he was finally able to open his mouth without a sob emerging, it was to ask the Commander, "How can you be so cruel?"

"This cruelty is a kindness," the Commander told him. "This is a good pain, like the disinfecting of a wound. You must remember it all, Fabrice. You must never forget. It is remembering that will ensure that you never pick up a weapon again. It is remembering that will make you safe when I am gone."

"But you cannot leave!" Fabrice protested. "I am not strong enough without you!"

"You were always stronger than you knew," the Commander responded. "And across the river, there are yet boys forced to fight men's wars. They need my help. They need me, Fabrice. They need us both."

Fabrice sat on his cot, knees folded under his chin. Outside the medical tent, one of the men in blue helmets gestured towards the tent's entrance. There were other men with him, men with cameras and with microphones, and also boys: Eshele and Gaussou. Fabrice heard snatches of their conversation and heard his name mentioned often. "Who are you?" he asked the voice.

"I was a soldier, Fabrice. I led men into battle, and later, to my shame, I led boys. I am one who killed many enemies, and whose actions led to the deaths of many friends. But death came for me, eventually, as is the way of war. And yet I did not die, but live on. And it is my fate, Fabrice, to be one with the children I once led into battle—to share the hardships and suffering that men like me once inflicted upon them. My soul bonds with that of a boy. I share his fate and his experiences. I share his pain. And I must live on in this fashion forever—or until twenty-four hours pass without a single child in this nation firing a weapon in anger. Until that event occurs, I can never rest."

"But . . . that is impossible," Fabrice said. "You have been set an impossible task."

"How does one eat an elephant, Fabrice?"

For the first time in weeks, Fabrice smiled. "One bite at a time," he responded.

"Yes. Just so."

"How can I help?"

"You may help by becoming a soldier in my army, Fabrice. By refusing to take up arms again. By telling the story of your life to all who will listen, for in this new war, your life is your weapon.

"And you may help by telling them about me, Fabrice. Spread the word to every corner of the nation, to every village and every camp. Let the boy soldiers know that the Commander is on the prowl, and that I am coming quickly to their aid, to be their partner and their shield.

"Who can say? It may be that, when my legend becomes known, the rules will change—that I am suddenly everywhere, all at once. That I am whispering simultaneously into the ears of many boys, speaking to them of their true strength, of what it truly is to be a man and to be a soldier. Whispering about who the true enemies are, and at whom the guns are to be pointed. Yes, just so.

"And tell the others, too. Tell the likes of Muteba. Yes. Tell them that the Commander is coming for them, as well.

"Tell them, Fabrice. Tell them the Commander is coming."

There was no twinkling of the air, no apparition of mist

or smoke appeared, to tell Fabrice when the Commander left him. Nor was there any diminution of his own new-found strength. There were only the men with cameras and microphones at his bedside, clicking away and asking their questions, and Fabrice greeted them with a smile.

What, after all, had Fabrice to fear? He was a man with a mission, ready to advance and fully in command.

Steve DuBois lives in Kansas City, where he teaches high school and coaches the school's debate, speech, and Quidditch teams. For more of his literary misadventures, check out www.stevedubois.net.

REFLECTIONS

Susan Bianculli

I'm running through a fun house mirror maze at night, but I don't know how I got here. What I do know is that several shadowy people are after me! My repeatedly screamed questions to them of "Why?" and "Leave me alone!" reverberate and bounce off the reflective surfaces around me until I can't hear myself think, never mind hear what answer is being yelled back to me.

I continue to run as fast as I can to get away from those who chase me. I should be panting, but I feel remarkably fine, like I could do this all night long. Hopefully my pursuers will tire and give up before I do. The low emergency lights that had been left on for the night in this maze glint off knives held in their hands. Their knives look remarkably like the knife I have pulled out of my purse for self-protection. Will they kill me if they catch me? I don't want to stop and find out. I've never used my knife before.

But the shadowy figures keep on hunting me—sometimes coming so close that a mere pane of glass or the thickness of a mirror separates us. I pray that some night guard on the premises will hear all the noise and come to rescue me from this crazy, narrow-halled labyrinth before my pursuers catch up. I bang off the tricky glass-and-mirrored-paneled hallways as I charge always forward at a frantic run, though weirdly I'm not feeling any pain when I hit. There has to be an exit somewhere, but the red lights make it all so confusing. I can't find the way out!

I trip, and I fall to the floor. I try to get up, but I can't. My body no longer responds to my mental urgings. All I can do is open my eyes. My red blood, made even more crimson by the nighttime illumination, spreads out beneath me; the knife I'd been holding sticks out from under me. Now I know why I can't move. I must have accidentally severed something deep inside me when I fell! I lie prone in the hallway, scared, counting the minutes until I can be discovered by someone. Thankfully, my pursuers have vanished.

The morning business lights are switched on, and I nearly cry with relief. I will be rescued! It takes a while, but soon some EMTs come with their gurneys to remove me and someone else's body to their ambulance. It seems I wasn't the only one running away in here last night. I spare a thought for the other poor unfortunate and blink against the brightening day as we are wheeled towards the entrance.

My relief changes to horror as I slowly wink out of existence when the gurney I am on passes the last mirrored panel at the beginning of the maze.

Susan Bianculli wears the titles "Mother" and "Wife" most proudly. Another is "Author" for her *The Mist Gate Crossings* series, as well as several short stories in several other anthologies besides this one. To learn about the other things she's had published, check out: susanbianculli.wix.com/home

EXILE

Bethany Marcello

War.
Raw.
The words seem to be about the same to me.
Both strip you to the very center and leave nothing
but hurt and pain. In the end, if you're very lucky,
there will be scars, scars that itch and pull and tear
but never fit as good as what was there before. You
can never be the same. You can never be as good.

I stand at the window. Chips crack the whitewashed frame. I run my finger along it and look beyond the glass, towards a field that lays at the edge of the farmhouse in which I stand. It's empty now, even though planting season has just started. Brown furrows should be lining that field, ready for the hard kernels of oats and barley, but I can only see grass, hardened by a too long winter.

Even though humans and the Lothari had been fighting for decades—ever since humans first settled on what the Lothari considered their land, but we consider New America, land given to us by the council after the War of Galactic Extermination—this last winter has crippled the humans. A dangerous disease called Endtre has decimated half of City-Settlement and even more in the countryside, where few can afford medicine.

I turn away from a world painted in dead winter grays towards Amber, my kid sister. She plays behind me with a doll, one Mama gave her the birthday before the government issued the banishing. Amber is absorbed by her doll's peach skin and red lips. She wraps her black-brown fingers around the doll's arm, steadying it gently to help it walk. I feel overwhelmed by my sister's gentleness.

Where does a seven-year-old learn that? I wonder. *Since the banishing it's been nothing but barely surviving, and yet here she shows more grace to a doll than I have shown her all day.*

"Amber, we need to check out the kitchen, grab a few more things before we leave," I say to her, brushing away my emotions. But my voice is gentler than normal.

As she stands up, she asks, "Is it much longer to City-Settlement? We've been walking for so long."

"Not much longer. Less than a day. We'll be there to-night."

"And will Mama be there?" she asks.

I look away from her coal-black eyes. "She'll be there."

"Good. I have so much to tell her. She'll be so proud of me."

"Very proud. I bet if we look hard enough in the kitchen we might find some special treats."

"Really?" Amber says. She walks over to me and catches my blistered hand in her own. I feel myself choking up over this little girl's trust in me.

We walk into the kitchen, a small space with a table and a coal stove, which sits empty in the corner. There are no windows in the room, just a difficult-to-see hatch along the wall, probably leading to the root cellar, and a taller door leading to the farmyard.

"Sarah, my favorite cookies are the ones with chocolate on top. They are my extra favorites. Do you see any of those?"

I open the closest cupboard. "No, I don't. There's not too much of anything in here, is there?" I say, looking around the sparse room. The former owners must have taken everything with them when the government banished people from living in the countryside surrounding the capital. An emerald beam catches my eye as a burst of sunlight streams from the parlor window and passes through a hidden glass jar.

"Strayberry preserves!" I say excitedly. "You love strayberries, Amber."

"I do?"

"Don't you remember? Mama made chortle cake and covered it with strayberries the two of you had picked from the hedges."

"No. But it sounds good," Amber said. "Not as good as chocolate cookies, though."

I reach up to the preserves, pulling them down to the splintery counter. It takes all my might, and I practically bend my fingernails in half, but I still manage to open the jar's band and lid. It releases with a satisfying snap.

"Look, a spoon," Amber says, finding a bent utensil in a drawer. We take turns licking the sticky, green jam.

"I really like this," Amber says. I smile and lean in, kissing the dark jam ringing her pink cheeks. I feel happy, something I haven't felt in a long time.

We finish the strayberry jam and rest the jar and spoon in the sink as if it were our house to keep clean and tidy, as if Mama and I would wash them together. Just as we load the last of the supplies—a few more jars of jam and pickled vegetables—into my pack, I turn to see the empty things in the sink, praying to whoever listens, that life could be as normal as dirty dishes and sweet jam again.

"Ready, Miss Amber?"

"Yes!"

Amber rushes through the farmhouse door and down the wooden steps, turning back to wave at me. I smile at her sugared energy and return the happy wave. I bend my knees to hoist the heavy pack a few inches higher on my hips.

I look up, terrified, at the sound of a bird call, a very specific bird call.

Lothari, I think.

My heart pounds. As calmly as I can, I turn to my sister. "Amber, I need you to come with me right now."

Amber must have heard the birdsong, too, because she turns to me, her eyes wide and shoulders small, already too thin from not getting enough to eat, not wanting to eat. With the pack, my movements are jerky, but we manage to get to the kitchen and down to the dark root cellar below.

Within minutes, heavy footsteps pound against the kitchen floor. The guttural sounds of the Lothari language roar across the room as I hear several natives hunt through the cupboards. It must be Lothari boundary guards raiding homesteads. Occasionally they could be kind and gentle, but often they were cruel. I didn't want to take a chance.

I hold Amber against me. I can feel every bit of her, bones and flesh, all tight with fear. I try to calm my heart and breathing, hoping that it comforts her. We both listen in the black-dark as footsteps hunt through the house.

The door to the cellar opens. The cellar is deep, unusual for a house this size. Amber and I are pushed as far back as the room allows. The light from above can't find us, and neither can the Lothari who is peering in. He eventually leaves. Silence invades the rest of the house.

I don't know how long I wait before peering out the cellar door, but it is dark outside. Quietly, carefully, I walk out of the root cellar and away from the house, Amber clasped tightly to my body. She is asleep, exhausted.

Constantly looking around, I make it to the edge of the barn and then the edge of the tall grass and then, finally, to the middle of the field. The moons are not out tonight, and so I walk in complete darkness. Each step is tentative and slow as I try to find my footing in the uneven soil.

I feel something slam against me, and I fall over, almost landing on Amber. She wakes up, crying, and I gently release her on the ground, throwing my pack behind her while reaching for the weapon strapped to my leg. It is a gun, probably from the War of Extermination, the only weapon I could find when we left our village.

In the dark I can't see anything, and Amber's crying makes it impossible to hear clearly. I take a few steps to my right when I am tackled again. This time, my head lands hard against a rock. My last thought before I lose consciousness is a memory of Amber and a kiss that tastes like strayberry jam.

I awake suddenly as though I had stopped breathing in my sleep. "Amber," I call out, remembering, though my vision is blurry.

"Sarah?" Amber says. She is at my side. It's now daytime, and we are hidden among the tall grasses, still in the middle of the field where we'd been attacked last night.

"You are all right?" I say, almost incredulous.

"Yes," she says, "All right." There are rocks in her hand.

"What happened?" I ask, shaking my head as I sit up.

"Sinar and I are playing a game."

"Sinar?" I ask. Then I see her. Symmetrical black dots pock gray-green skin. The aliens—natives as the settlers call them, Lothari as they call themselves—bear a strong resemblance to humans, but the colors are all wrong. They wear white, sleeveless robes and each has a small, black bird that sings eerie songs as a companion. It is that birdsong that alerted me to danger yesterday.

I see a yellow stripe down the front of the sleeveless robe, running all the way to the Lotharian girl's feet. *Capture, slave,* I think.

Sinar, as Amber calls her, must have followed my eyes because she says, "I ran away." Her chin rises defiantly.

Surprise widens my eyes and mouth, surprise and

fear. Any Lothari capture caught running away is flayed alive, their body stretched as wide as a doorway. I have heard rumors that the death of a runaway is only slightly worse than the life.

The alien sits in front of a small mound of stacked rocks, her elbows on her knees. "You were going to run right off that cliff," she says, her voice low. She points. To my horror, I see the telltale outline of jagged rocks, blue sky, and nothing else. It's a ravine with a river far below that would have killed Amber and me long before we landed. A broken fence slat swings in the wind.

"Sinar did not mean to hurt you, Sarah," said Amber. "She was trying to help."

"Thanks," I say, begrudgingly.

"Your sister was scared in the night. So I stayed."

"Thanks," I say again. I touch my head to my eyes, trying to rub away the blurriness.

"Can Sinar come with us to City-Settlement?" Amber asks, her hand against my knee as she pushes herself to stand. We are face to face as I sit on the ground, my head still aching from the fall. We are covered in the dry dust of this desert planet, our dresses more dun than any other color, and yet the Lothari capture looks as though she just walked away from a bathhouse.

"I'm sure the Lothari would find life in City-Settlement . . .," I say, not sure how to finish.

"Are you running from the banishing?" Sinar asks in the silence.

"Our village was destroyed by the Endtre virus," I say.

"And it will be sprayed, and you go to your capital?" she asks. Her all-black eyes watch mine.

To rid our land of the disease, the government created a spray that was extremely poisonous. It causes immediate deformations and death. But it is the only known way to destroy the virus, which is even deadlier. It takes three years for the spray to disappear from the land completely. The government banished everyone in the villages, for our safety, they said. My sister and I, like all the others were headed to City-Settlement to live.

Everyone who lives in the city, even the refugees, commit themselves to isolation for twenty-one days, long enough to prove they're not contagious. But once inside the capital, life is cramped in the refugee camps, very uncomfortable. Many are poor, and there is little work. Those that had always lived in City-Settlement resent the newcomers, and the strain of so many on resources already destroyed by famine, disease, and years of war with the Lothari make tensions extremely fraught. Living in the capital for the three years it would take to make our village liveable is an overwhelming prospect, but it's the only one my sister and I have.

Even worse, I had told Amber that Mama was waiting

for us in City-Settlement, but Mama had seen the signs in herself, signs she'd seen from our father—fever, headache, red eyes. She had immediately fled in hopes Amber and I might be safe. Only five days had passed since we left Montesa, our village, another seventeen days before I'd know for sure if we were safe.

"Are you sick?" the Lothari asks.

For some reason, the virus doesn't affect the Lothari, not like it does humans. They get sick but rarely die. For humans, Endtre has an almost 100% fatality rate. There are rumors that the Lothari developed the virus and then passed it to humans by sharing contaminated blankets with those seeking aid.

"No," I say.

"They won't let you into your capital if you are," Sinar says.

"I know," I say. I wish she wouldn't talk about serious things in front of Amber. "Was that hunting party after you?"

"No. No one is after me," Sinar says.

We know then that the other lied. The Lothari's bird, smaller than my thumb and with black feathers of iridescent green, lands on her shoulder, returning from an overhead flight. Sinar whistles to it, and the bird flies to Amber, dancing around her. She laughs happily.

The two small ones continue their play. Looking at the bird, Sinar says softly, so Amber can't hear, "I can help you."

"How?"

"I can help you get to your capital, avoid the hunting parties. I know this land. You do not. You still have three days ahead of you."

"Three? It can't be more than half a day to City-Settlement."

"If you had followed the road. But you have gotten yourself lost."

I had avoided the roads because Lothari hunting parties, looking to raid refugees on their way to City-Settlement, had greatly increased since the banishing. Amber and I only had another ten days before the government sent skyships filled with spray. I couldn't afford to get lost.

"And what do you get out of this?" I ask. I look down at a brown blade of grass. It's flat and as wide as my thumb with blue stripes down its front.

"I want to go home. You will pretend that I am your capture for any Triora that cross us," she says, using the Lothari word for humans, "and I'll help you avoid hunting parties as well as guide you."

Where Lothari captured each other and humans in battle and used them as slaves, humans used captured Lothari as servants, giving them freedom after seven years of work. It wasn't unbelievable that a refugee would bring a Lothari still serving a sentence to the capital.

I look to Sinar. *Does she realize selling a Lothari capture in City-Settlement would set up Amber and me for much longer than the three years we'd need to wait out the spray? It would buy us wooden walls instead of a tent shared jealously with four other families, food instead of supplements, medicine, safety, certainty—even enough to rebuild our small farm in Montesa,* I think.

"If you can avoid hunting parties, you can avoid humans," I say.

"Your people do not smell the same, do not move the same. Only skilled warriors find them. I am not skilled in such a way. There will be many Triora the closer I am to your capital. "

"You found me. You could have avoided me."

"You ran barely two feet away from me while I was sleeping in the grass. That I couldn't see you shows I am vulnerable," she say.

"You want to go to the capital?" I asked.

"No, I want to go home. But I need you to travel safely through your lands, which I will be entering very soon. My village is only a few hours' walk from the capital."

I know it is a good plan—or at least better than what I had. "I don't trust you," I say.

Sinar smiles to herself, her lips a darkish green. There is little humor in her expression. "I don't trust you."

We spend the rest of the day walking through the dusty land, a hot sky overhead, and sand below. Sinar stops us to make camp at a small, brown creek, just beyond the border between human and Lothari land. She talks little throughout the day, though I occasionally catch her smiling softly to Amber, who seems fascinated by the Lothari. It is rare that anyone from our village had seen a native, unless of course they were sent by the government to a neverending battlefield. But then, it's even rarer to come back from the war to tell of what a Lothari was like.

As night drapes over us and Amber is tucked into our bedroll, ready to drift into sleep, I spy the purple smoke of fire in the distance from other banished villagers.

I look over to Amber, her eyes drooping softly. "They must be burning yuclo vines," I say to Amber. "Do you remember when we burned those on last Shabatz Day?"

"Mama would set off fireworks and make special treats. They must be celebrating," Amber says smiling. "Do you have yuclo vines, Sinar?"

"Yes, they are also quite special to us. We often use them for wedding ceremonies," Sinar says.

"What are Lothari weddings like?" Amber asks.

"Quiet, soulful," she says, her eyes downcast.

"Have you ever been to a ceremony?"

"Yes," she says. "My own ceremony."

"You were married?" I ask. She is older than me but doesn't look it.

"Yes. Milu. My husband. He watches over our son. It

is them that I return to."

"We lost our Mama, too," says Amber. "But she is waiting for us in the capital."

I see tears in Sinar's eyes as she looks at first Amber, then me. I look back to the purple smoke in the sky.

The next day passes the same, walking and then stopping to make camp. Sinar stops us this time, not at a creek, but at a small monument, little more than a pillar of rocks and a metal plaque cemented to the ground.

"We will stop here at Bett-Shay. Do you know what Bett-Shay is?" Sinar says.

I look at her face, but her expression is closed.

Amber holds my hand and studies the monument. I look closely and see, engraved on the plaque, images of Captains Bett and Shay, who had piloted the first ships from Earth sixty years ago. Beyond the miniscule memorial is a wide, flat land of high desert. In the distance jagged cliffs stretch across the sky, where I can see the very tops of the crystal domes that protect City-Settlement from disease and war.

"Here is where humans first landed on this planet," I say. "During the Wars of Extermination, Earth was destroyed, our people held prisoner . . . and worse. After, the Galactic Council gave us this planet to make a new home."

Sinar looks at me over the monument. "When humans first landed in Lothari, we were cautious. Could we find friends here? But then you started digging the wells miles below the earth that destroyed the water that had existed since there were Lothari. My people went thirsty and died while yours went swimming. This place is not a good place for my people. Is it for yours?"

"We wanted a home," I say.

"So you took ours?"

I don't have an answer. I turn back to the camp and prepare the fire for dinner.

"Only another day until you are where you want to be," Sinar says.

The next day we prepare for our last walk until we reach the capital. Amber is again playing with the Lothari's bird when the native comes to my side. "Your mother, does she really wait at the capital?"

I continue stuffing my pack with our bedrolls and supplies, not looking up.

"What makes you think she isn't?"

"Your sister talks about your mother, and you look away from her."

"No, she is not at the capital. My mother has the virus."

"So she is dead, or soon will be."

"Yes." It is hard to say this word, harder than it has ever been to say a word.

"You will have to tell your sister," Sinar says. "The wound you delay giving her is made worse when she learns her sister deceived her."

A sound behind me draws my attention, and I know before I see that Amber is behind me. Her black skin is dark against her ragged pink sweater. "You are talking about Mama," Amber says. "Tell me."

"Amber, now is not the time." My voice is gruff. I am terrified of this moment, of what I have to do.

"Tell me. I know something is wrong. But you won't say it. Just say it!"

I remain motionless, frozen by her pain and mine.

Amber turns back, runs away, towards the bluff, towards the crystal-dome.

I throw down my pack and run after her. Sinar stands back. From far away, I see Amber trip and fall. She rolls frantically down a massive, scrubby hill.

"Amber!" I shout.

At the top of the hill, I can see Amber's small body below, unnaturally still. I can also, in the far, far distance, see a sandy valley made white by the robes of a massive army. What looks like the whole of Lothari waits just beyond the sight of the sparkling domes of City-Settlement. Blood-rage fills the air as the warriors wait to crash their weapons against bodies.

They will destroy us, I realize. *They will wait at our borders, shoot down any aid ships from the Galactic Council, and let us starve from within. It is hopeless. It has always been hopeless.*

I rush to Amber's side. She is breathing steadily but is not awake. Keeping her still, I gently touch her head for wounds. Her eyes flutter lightly at my touch, and she wakes.

"Sarah?" she says.

I cry, relieved and even more terrified, now that I can be. I lean down to kiss her cheek and stroke hair from her forehead. "What hurts? What can I do?"

She lifts herself up, slowly, painfully. "I don't know what happened. I . . .."

I see the exact moment she remembers. She looks at me. "Is it true, Sarah?" Her voice seems tinier than she is. I nod, tears threatening my eyes. She reaches for me, as she did when she was very little and had fallen, certain her sister could make the hurt go away. Great sobs tear my heart open.

"We must leave this place," Sinar says, leaning down next to us in the sand. There is fear in her voice but not surprise.

I stand up. "You knew about this," I say, pointing to the army below. Black dots swarm in the sky above the military camp, the Lothari birds.

"The spray will destroy our land as well as yours. I can take you to the doors of the capital. I know another way," Sinar says.

Rage rips through me. I stand up and away from

Amber and pull the gun secured at my leg, pointing it at Sinar. "You knew about this! You knew that your people were going to attack mine, completely wiping us from memory. What was the point of helping Amber and me? Easing your conscious by putting a pause on our death sentence? Do you know how much I could get for selling you in the Capture-Market. Enough to outwait any seige you Lothari would throw at us!"

"Don't do this, Sarah. Don't let this be the price you pay for Amber's safety," Sinar says, her hands in the air.

"I am tired of fighting, of being right. I miss Mama. I want to be safe. Amber deserves that. She deserves so much more than a life spent at the edges. I left Montesa so she could have more, have that. What happens when you have a child and you can't be wrong?"

"This is not the way," Sinar said. I see fear in her eyes. Amber is at my feet, whimpering. "Please, Sarah, don't do this," Sinar says, "I have a child. Don't make him motherless."

I look down at Amber. *I can't keep her from destruction,* I think, *not when we hide in a cellar, not when I bring her to the capital that is supposed to save us, nothing. I can't protect her.* I drop the gun and collapse in tears. *I am only fourteen. I know too much of death. My whole life is a scar.* I fall to my knees, defeated.

Sinar comes to me, puts her hand on my shoulder.

"We cannot undo the war between our people. But we can undo the war between ourselves. Come home with me. I cannot promise you safety, but I can give you a home."

Amber leans close and snuggles her cheek against mine. "I love you, Sarah." She stays close, her body warm and small and fragile. "You are my home."

I cry harder. It is the first time I have cried since we left Montesa and Mama.

"Let hope anchor you, Sarah, not sorrow," Sinar says. She kneels next to me. Heavier than it has ever been, my body rises from the sand as Amber and Sinar help me stand. I follow them into the desert. I am done with hoping. I am done with war.

Bethany Marcello loves puns, pugs and playing pretend. She has held many jobs, including popcorn popper, bubble salesman and, most illogical of all, middle school teacher. She currently lives in a 100-year-old farmhouse in the hills of Pennsylvania with her high school sweetheart of a husband and young daughter. You can probably find her in the garden growing orange watermelons, in the kitchen baking organic rustic bread or lost in a good story.

BEYOND THE PROMISED LAND

Darrel Duckworth

Jond's heart pounded in his ears as he buried his axe in Rolf's skull. He felt bone crunch and blood splatter his face as the blade drove through. Rolf's eyes sprung wide in pain and horror just before his body collapsed to the ground. Tearing his axe free, Jond roared out his victory cry.

For a second, he saw Gunnar fiercely grinning in approval. Then the older man was lost in the press of bodies. Shaking a tangle of hair from his face, Jond leapt into the heart of the melee, crashing his axe against the shield of the next opponent.

That evening, Rolf avoided him, sitting and sulking far from him at the Great Table. Catching his attention, Jond raised his goblet, a salute to a good opponent. Rolf shot him an angry glare, then turned his head away.

"Forget it," Gunnar advised. "Rolf is also new here. He still takes defeat personally. In time he will come to understand."

"Perhaps I need to split his skull a few more times to help him understand," Jond said, angered at the slight.

"Don't get too arrogant, pup," the older warrior warned. "You are good, but perhaps tomorrow he will split yours."

Jond laughed.

Gunnar shook his head, smiling patiently.

They drank and wenched themselves into exhaustion and slept.

The next day, Rolf was killed before Jond even caught sight of him. It didn't matter. There was plenty of battle to be had, and Jond enjoyed it to its fullest. Against so many, more-experienced warriors, he was forced to draw on all his strength and skill just to survive. It was exhilarating.

His large axe gave him an advantage. It was a hard weapon to defend against. For most men, a large, heavy axe was a clumsy weapon—difficult to use in close combat. To Jond, it felt like a part of his arm. He swung, jabbed, and blocked with it easier than most men did with much smaller weapons.

Indeed, with his axe in hand and his blond hair brushing the muscles of his broad shoulders, Jond knew that he was the true image of a Viking. In life, some of his clan, while deep in their cups, had even gone so far as to compare him to the thunder god . . . in appearance at least. Jond had done his best to live up to—and die with—that image. In a short but glorious life, he had been a fierce and respected warrior. In the end, it had taken three enemies to kill him, and two of those, he was sure, went to their own gods shortly after him.

But that was in another life although, sometimes, he thought of his final moments on Midgard . . . and the Valkyrie who had carried him to this land-after-death.

He had risen from the ground, feeling strong but strange. Then he had looked down onto his own body, his face crushed, his head half-hacked from his shoulders and his body chalk white except for the gaping wounds. The sight of his death had shaken him in a way that he still denied though the image would not leave his mind.

Around him and unaware of him, his living kinsmen had rested, recovering from the battle. Others of his clan rose up from their bodies as he had and stood looking around in the same daze that he felt.

Then a motion caught his eyes, and he'd looked up to see the Valkyrie riding down from the clouds on their winged horses. One of them had landed and stopped right next to him. He'd looked up at her, full and beautiful in her armor, her tightly-braided hair pulled back from her strong face. She was perfect beauty.

He had stared, unable to speak.

She had seemed to understand. She'd smiled at him.

"Pick up your weapon, warrior," she'd said. "You will have need of it."

He had bent and grabbed his axe, then he mounted the horse behind her. He had gripped her tightly as the horse launched from the earth and they rose into the sky leaving Midgard far below. Inside the clouds, the sky became an endless, shifting grey, yet horse and rider had ridden on as though they could see their destination clearly.

At last, the swirling fog had parted, and the horse's hooves had sounded on solid ground again. They slowed to a trot and stopped before a huge, looming set of doors set into a grey, stone wall. A dozen feet to either side of the doors, the wall had blended into the swirling fog.

"Through those doors is your future, Jond," the Valkyrie had said, looking over her shoulder at him. "I must return to Midgard to bring others."

Indeed, even as they had talked, two more Valkyrie arrived with men from the battle. Jond had dismounted and stood next to the horse, looking up at her beauty.

"Will I see you again?" he'd asked.

She had looked at him a moment, as if deciding his worthiness.

"Perhaps. That is your decision."

With that, she had turned and galloped into the fog. Jond and the others had pushed open the great doors, entered Valhalla, and joined in their first of endless battles.

Now, he stood among this day's battle. He shook himself from the memory of the Valkyrie's beauty and returned his mind to the fight. To die because he was dreaming of a woman, even one of the Valkyrie, would be an embarrassment that would not soon be forgotten. Deflecting his next opponent's blade, he lunged in and killed him.

The next day, Jond found himself fighting side by side with Rolf. The two threw aside their bitterness to fight together against the common foe. Together they fought. Together they fell. That night, they drank together and talked as friends. Gunnar looked on, pleased.

Jond caved in Rolf's ribs, crashing through to his heart. He stepped past Rolf's twitching body to engage the next man.

Jond felt the fire burn inside him as the blade sliced his belly open and his entrails spilled out.

Rolf smiled at him as he fell.

"At last, I kill you, friend."

Darkness closed in from the edges of Jond's eyes as he watched Rolf step over him to engage another man. He reached up with his hand to grab Rolf's boot, but he was too weak, and his hand was kicked aside. He fell into the darkness.

He and Gunnar tested each other, probing and feinting. Then they crashed together. Only one moved on to another foe.

The battle done, Jond screamed out his victory cry. Nearby, Rolf joined him. Gunnar laughed and wiped his blade clean on a body.

Time passed without passing. Glorious Time, filled with the strength of men's arms in battle and their laughter around the Great Table. Time passed with the ring of metal on metal, the clunk of goblets on wooden tables, and the cooing of warm maidens in the night. Time passed, and Jond watched the ranks of Valhalla swell.

Gunnar?" Jond slurred, the ale numbing his tongue. "Hmmmm?"

"Have you ever wondered . . . what is the . . . reason for Valhalla? What it is for?"

"What?" the older man asked drunkenly. His heavy-lidded eyes continued to stare out into the almost-empty Great Hall where they sat on the floor swilling ale, buttocks on the cold stone, backs against the cold stone wall. Most of the others had left already for wenching or sleep.

"Some say that this is the reward for those who fall as heroes," Jond said. "Others say that it is a training ground. That the greatest are taken here after their death to fight endlessly, honing their skills so that they can fight for Odin when Ragnarok comes."

Gunnar nodded drunkenly, in complete agreement.

"You have been here longer than most, old man," Jond said. "What do you think?"

"I think that the gods do not care what I think. We are here now . . . and now this is all there is for us. Forget your dreams of glory, pup. Forget about fighting with Odin and Thor against Ragnarok. It is not named the End of All Things by chance. Think only of now. Live this second life you have been given. Live it full . . . while you have it."

"While I have it?" Jond asked. "What are you talking about? We will live forever here. No man dies in Valhalla."

Gunnar snorted a laugh.

"In one breath you talk of Ragnarok, and in the next you babble about living forever. You know nothing of what you speak."

The old man lifted his cup to his lips but didn't drink.

He stared into it and spoke in a hollow voice.

"Heroes die in Valhalla, Jond."

Jond felt his anger rising. He turned drunkenly to argue, but the words died in his throat when he looked into the old man's eyes. Those eyes sent a frozen arrow into his heart.

For the first time since his boyhood, Jond felt fear. Fear for his old friend. Fear for a man who was so like a father to him.

Gunnar's words were not the harsh words of a rebuking elder; they were the tired words of one who would go soon. Jond had been here long enough to have seen a warrior leave. The words echoed in his mind.

Heroes die in Valhalla.

He slumped back against the cold stone and drank his cup dry.

So it came. Time passed without passing, as always. Gunnar fought with the same skill and strength, but his spirit faded a little each day. Jond watched as the old warrior fell in battle more and more often, more a victim of himself than his foe.

A man without heart did not last long in battle.

Then came the day they faced each other again.

Jond finished his foe. Turning to grapple with the next man, he found himself facing Gunnar.

Hesitation stretched out between them, a fragile calm amid the storm.

Stunned, Jond watched Gunnar slowly lower his weary sword. The young warrior followed the elder's gaze down to his own battleaxe. Jond saw only the normal gore of battle on the blade and haft, but when he looked up again, it seemed that Gunnar's eyes saw something more.

Those old eyes looked up again.

Gunnar shook his head slightly.

Shocked, Jond watched him turn away. Fear shot through his belly. If Gunnar was ready to leave battle, he would be ready to leave Valhalla. That was how it always happened.

He charged the older man.

Gunnar sensed the charge and stopped, waiting for the blow without turning.

Jond swept his axe by, inches from Gunnar's head and shoulder.

The old man nodded, still without turning, then stepped away.

A wave of battle swept in and caught Jond up, pushing him away from Gunnar.

Jond remembered little after that: only blind, angry bloodlust. When it passed, he found himself kneeling in the gore cradling Gunnar's mangled form, hot tears streaming down his cheeks. No one came near them.

Jond ate without feasting that evening. Rolf sat on his right. An empty chair sat on his left.

Around the table, others tried to carry on as though nothing had happened, but he knew they felt the heaviness in their hearts too. Gunnar had been one of the oldest and best-liked here. He had been a true Viking.

The ceremony ran itself through Jond's mind again, unbidden and unwanted. It had taken place as soon as all could stand again, as was the custom. Here the spirit could not leave the flesh as it had on Midgard, for they were, in fact, spirit made flesh. Here, death was a decision, a surrender.

The tables had been pushed against the walls, and the host of heroes had assembled themselves on either side of the Great Hall, leaving a wide corridor up the middle. Gunnar's closest friends stood near the end.

From that end, Jond watched as the old warrior entered through the distant doors and laid his shield and sword at the foot of the Hallmaster. Then he began the long walk up the aisle between warriors. One after the next, they each turned their backs as he approached, shunning him in his shame and cowardice. Some turned away in anger. Some turned away reluctantly.

Jond watched Gunnar walk steadily up the human corridor. There was no shame in the set of the old man's shoulders, just weariness. He walked toward the tapestry at the end of the Hall.

To Jond's left, Rolf hesitantly lowered his head and turned away.

Jond remained facing forward, watching Gunnar close the final steps between them. His eyes locked with the old man's.

Jond burned the pity from his heart. Gunnar had come here as a hero many years before Jond had even been born. He would not insult his friend now in his final moments.

The Hallmaster walked the required two paces behind Gunnar and Jond felt the huge man's hot glare ordering him to turn away.

He set his shoulders and refused. To the grey realms of Hel with the Hallmaster. Jond's father had died at sea, not as a hero, when Jond was a young boy, and Jond had never seen him again. He would not turn his back on Gunnar who was so like a father to him.

The old man stopped in front of him and looked into his eyes. Gunnar smiled a little and gripped Jond's arm.

Jond gripped Gunnar's in return. This time, Jond held back his tears.

Gunnar's smile faded and, in the old man's eyes, Jond saw . . . pity?

Then Gunnar nodded and turned to face the end of the hall.

The Hallmaster walked past them and drew the tapestry aside, revealing a small door. He unbarred the door and swung it open, exposing the swirling, grey fog beyond.

Jond watched Gunnar's shoulders rise and fall with a deep, final breath. Then he watched his friend walk through the door and be swallowed by the greyness. Jond felt as if he were choking.

It would have been better if Gunnar had never risen after falling in that last battle. Now he was nothing, not even a shade in Hel.

The Hallmaster closed and barred the door, then swung the tapestry back to hide it again.

Jond turned his back on the angry glare of the Hallmaster and stalked down the corridor of warriors, leaving before the Hallmaster could speak the ritual words denouncing Gunnar.

No one turned their back on Jond as he passed.

The battles came with the days and passed with them. For a time, Jond fought more fiercely, and angrily, than ever. But, eventually, Valhalla returned to its routine, and Jond just fought.

There have been no new arrivals for some time," Rolf said quietly, chewing on a roasted bird's leg.

"So?" Jond asked, washing his own food down with

a swallow from yet another of the endless goblets of ale.

"So? Do you not wonder what is happening on Midgard that there are no new heroes?"

"Perhaps our people are in a time of peace. It is no concern. Soon their blood will call them to battle again."

"What if it is not that?" Rolf asked. "What if Ragnarok has come? What if Midgard is no more?"

"If Ragnarok, the End of All Things, has come, how can we be sitting here eating burnt birds and talking nonsense?"

"Everyone knows that Valhalla is special, made with a part of Odin and Hel both. Perhaps Ragnarok came too quickly, and Odin could not call us forth to fight at his side. Perhaps we are all there is now."

Jond guzzled his ale.

"Well?" Rolf asked.

"Well, what?"

"By Odin's Eye, Jond! What do you think?"

"I think that neither the gods nor Ragnarok care what I think! What does it matter if we are the last? We were here for eternity before; we are here for eternity now. We can do nothing about it until eternity is done."

Rolf fell silent then. Jond finished his meal in that silence, then looked around for a woman to bed. Changing his mind, he got drunker and fell asleep alone.

The battles and days passed—meaningless without seasons, empty without cause.

Jond fought.

Others walked beyond the tapestry.

And still, Jond fought.

He sat in the Great Hall, staring at yet another roasted bird.

Thoughts crept into his mind. He tried to push them out, but they returned again and again.

He thought of the day's battle, and the day's before, and the many days before that. He thought of tomorrow's battle, and all the tomorrows beyond it, stretching off beyond sight into infinity.

Into eternity.

He stared at his food and ale, untouched on the Great Table before him.

Why had they fought today? Why would they fight tomorrow?

Eternity was a long time to fight without cause.

Jond stared into that eternity, seeing the days and battles stretch off into a distance that couldn't be seen. Endless. Meaningless. He saw and decided.

He stood.

Heads nearby turned toward him, expecting a drunken toast.

He stepped over the bench and retrieved his axe and shield from the wall.

Excited murmurs ran along the table. Jond was going to challenge someone! As word passed down, more heads turned to see who would be challenged.

Jond turned back and laid shield and axe on the huge oaken table.

Cold silence gripped his section of the room.

It spread like a slow wave down the table, then washed outward, spreading over all who sat in the Great Hall, smothering all sound.

He looked around at the men nearest him. In their eyes, he saw that a few of them would also make the same decision soon. In others, he saw the same weariness growing but held back by their fear of the grey nothingness beyond the door. He stepped back from the bench and turned toward the tapestries.

Rolf grabbed his arm.

"Jond! No."

Jond wrenched his arm free and walked toward the covered door. At the head of the tables, he saw the Hallmaster rise and move to intercept him. They met at the end of the tables, only a few feet from the door . . . only a few feet from where Jond and Gunnar had last stood together.

"You are drunk," the Hallmaster said. "Sit down again

and make your decision in the morning. See how the call of battle changes your mind."

Jond shook his head sharply.

The Hallmaster was a large man. He set himself solidly in Jond's path, hands at his side but ready.

"Then there must be the ceremony. You will wait until the others have eaten and moved the tables back. Then you may face your decision properly."

Amazement crept through Jond's weariness. It brought a tight smile to his lips. He almost laughed.

It amazed him that—in this moment—the Hallmaster thought ritual and ceremony meant anything to him. His fist lashed out and crushed the man's bull throat.

The Hallmaster crumpled to his knees, choking for air.

Jond stepped past him without concern. In the morning, the man would rise again and be ready for battle.

In the shock and confusion, Jond covered the few feet to the tapestry.

A cry went up behind him, but he was already tearing the tapestry from the cold, stone wall. He heard footfalls racing toward him. He grabbed the heavy bar and lifted, throwing it aside. The footsteps stopped as the thick, wooden board bounced on the floor. He smiled thinly, grimly amused that men who faced pain and death daily could fear something as simple as a door. He grabbed the cold handle and pulled.

He stood staring at the greyness beyond, and for a moment, he hesitated.

Then he remembered the endless fighting.

Tomorrow, it would begin again. And again. Ever again.

He stepped into the swirling grey.

Unreplenished from Midgard, the ranks of Valhalla shrank by one more.

Jond found himself swallowed by a wet, grey fog. It swirled and flowed all around him, even under his feet, though the ground felt solid beneath him. He looked over his shoulder, but the door and wall were gone. More grey swirled behind him. Perhaps this was Hel's underworld. If so, he welcomed it. Here he would fade into an uncaring shade—the empty spirit he was.

He stepped forward, ready to begin the aimless, endless wandering and forgetting . . .

. . . and emerged into a strange land.

It stretched on, seemingly endlessly. And it was filled with people. Many people.

Several stood near him, almost lined up side-by-side, looking around with the same confusion he felt.

Just a few feet to his left, a woman magically stepped out of a large, grey hole. She also stopped and looked around in confusion. The grey hole began closing behind her.

Jond looked behind him just in time to see a small, grey hole shrink to a dot and disappear. Apparently, he had arrived here by the same magic.

"I've been waiting a long time for you to make the decision," a voice said in front of him.

He spun back and found himself facing the Valkyrie who had brought him to Valhalla.

She stood before him in a loose-fitting tunic of light green, white leggings and sandals. Her blonde hair settled loosely on her shoulders, unbound.

He stared at her.

She smiled and held out her hand.

"Come," she said. "Everything will be explained."

"Where are we?" he asked. He saw the other arrivals also being met by someone. Farther in, many were walking in a loose, long procession headed somewhere.

"A common area that is kept plain to ease the transition from the different afterlives," she said.

"Transition? Afterlives?"

She nodded. "Most people are not ready to move on until they've spent enough time in their version of the 'land beyond death.' When they finally tire of 'paradise' or 'hell' or whatever they were taught to expect, they reject it. Then, they are finally ready to open up to less Earthly concepts and learn what really awaits."

He stared at her. None of this made sense.

"Come," she said, taking his hand. "Let me show you."

"How did you know I would be here?"

"It's my task to bring people. I asked to know when you would be coming."

"But who could tell you that?"

She smiled.

"You ask more questions than you used to, Jond. Hopefully, that means you're ready to learn. I could say 'the gods' but that isn't really correct. It's easier to show you than explain it."

She stepped back, tugging gently on his hands.

Wearily, he resisted. Even if it meant losing her, he could not return to more violence.

"I am not worthy to walk in the halls of the gods. I have left Valhalla. I have fallen."

The weathered lines of her face softened. She reached out and caressed his cheek.

"No one falls here," she said softly. "And there is so much more than you've been told."

He looked into her soft, blue eyes and saw that she was not mocking him.

For just a moment, something touched his heart, licking at weary wounds.

She gently pulled his hands, and he followed . . . into a world that was more than he had been promised . . . more than he had dreamed.

After a long career in high tech **Darrel Duckworth** returned to his first love, writing. He now spends more time on other worlds, occasionally returning to Earth to refill his coffee mug. His stories can be found in magazines such as *LORE*, *Bards and Sages*, and *Plasma Frequency* and in other anthologies such as *Coven* and *Wild Things*.

JAR OF PICKLES

by Sarah Lyn Eaton

Foster's stomach growled. He opened the fridge before he remembered that his mother had been going to the store after work. He found some forgotten, moldy cheese in the crisper drawer and a jar of kosher pickles behind some leftovers he wouldn't touch. He shuddered. *Meatloaf, gross.* He glanced up at the clock on the wall, the second hand still ticking around. It was three o'clock.

His stomach gurgled again and he pulled the jar of pickles out of the fridge. It was a good start. Setting them on the counter, he stepped over the empty dog food bowl to check the cupboards. The streaks of green paint on the outside of his wrist screamed against the white cabinets. He'd been painting trees onto plywood. Foster turned the sink faucet on and scrubbed his hands clean.

He was hungry. In the pantry he found an unopened

jar of peanut butter, and the starved army in his stomach began to riot. He unscrewed the cap and peeled the safety seal off as the buttery smell assaulted his nose. He sighed blissfully and grabbed a spoon from the dish rack. Scooping up a big dollop, he stuck it into his mouth.

His lips closed around the roasted nutty spread. His eyes rolled back in his head. The army of hungry soldiers in his gut quieted, tongues stuck to roofs of mouths. Foster shook his dark hair out of his eyes and savored it while rooting through the cupboard. He found unopened bags of tuna fish, as well as cans of hash, ravioli, and green beans with flip-top lids. None of it actually needed to be heated up. Score.

Foster tucked the jar of pickles under his arm and carried it into the living room. His foot came down on something soft and fleshy and his stomach flip-flopped anxiously. He lifted his foot gently and the resounding squeak of the dog toy pierced the air. The glass slipped from the crook of his elbow and the boy yelped, leaping backwards.

The jar shattered the quiet in the house, soon permeating the air with the scent of pickling preservatives. Without thinking, Foster grabbed a gallon Ziploc bag from the drawer behind him and began to pick the pickles out of the melee of glass chunks. Five second rule, he smirked, sealing the bag tightly.

He left the puddle of pickle juice and stepped around the broken glass, feeling foolish for being startled. He closed the peanut butter jar and licked the spoon clean. Foster glanced up at the clock again. It was quarter after three.

Jill lifted herself up from her purple quilt. *It's time to get moving,* she sighed, rubbing the well-worn velvet patches beneath her fingers. She unrolled a thick pair of wool socks and pulled them on. They were better for hiking, she thought, unsure of how far she'd be walking.

She finished dressing, shedding her dirty top for a soft and warm sweater. She inhaled the faint scent of lavender dryer sheets. Jill brushed her damp carrot-colored hair before braiding it tightly and dropped the brush into her backpack. She moved quickly around her bedroom, grabbing an extra sports bra and pair of underwear, as well as her favorite tee and flannel shirt.

She rummaged beneath the bathroom sink for her box of tampons, and she snagged a bottle of mouthwash, deodorant, and her toothbrush. She smiled at the ratty stuffed unicorn on her bed and the dance medals pinned to her wall. She looked around her bedroom one last time.

Downstairs in the kitchen, Jill filled her water bottle and clipped it to her backpack. She took the boxes of meal bars she used for practices from the cupboard next to the fridge and dumped them into her bag. There was just enough room left for her to roll up the chenille afghan from the couch and shove it in, squeezing the zipper together to close it. Done. She hefted it onto her shoulders. It wasn't as heavy as she thought it would be.

The air smelled stale. No, not stale exactly. It was more like a moment on pause, frozen in time. The longer she stayed in its stillness, the stronger that sense seemed and the less the wooden walls felt like home.

She stood outside the basement door. Her hand landed lightly on the knob, but she didn't try to turn it. She leaned against the wood as she pulled her boots on. She hadn't opened any of the closed doors in the house. And she wasn't going to. There was no sound on the other side of them, and that was all right. It was better to leave while the house was still quiet.

Foster let his front door slam shut behind him. It thundered in the quiet neighborhood. No lawn mowers sounded. No birds called out. He shoved the plastic baggie of pickles into his backpack on top of the cans and looked up as another door closed, echoing against the slow burning sound in the mounds of rubble marking the street. Jill paused beside the charred remains of her family's Subaru. Their eyes met, and she nodded quietly.

She toed at the bits of debris in what had been a modest neighborhood. Foster crossed to her. They'd been surprised to find their neighborhood untouched. The next block over was a ruin, the blackened timbers still hot, scorching the air they were breathing.

"Anyone?" he asked, getting closer.

She didn't speak but shook her head no. She reached out and touched his wrist, where he'd removed the green paint. They'd been building sets for the school musical when the bombs started. After digging their way out of the basement, they had found an empty world.

"Which way do you think people went?" she wondered. Foster shrugged. Together, they faced away from the blackened block and started to walk.

Sarah Lyn Eaton is a writer fond of magical realism and dystopias. She has previously published the stories "The White Sisters" in *What Follows* and "Hold the Door" in *The Northlore Series, Volume 1: Folklore.*

THRESHOLD

Anthony R. Cardno

They've been goofing around in the backyard, just Callie and Billy Taugent and Kevin Collucci. Compared to slim, scrawny Callie, Billy and Kevin are big boys—teenage-bulky, on that border between chubby and musclebound. Imposing to Callie, but they wanted to hang out, and she so rarely has anyone include her anymore. Her parents are at work, but they wouldn't care that she has boys over. So she'd said sure.

Climbing the decrepit tree in the corner of the yard, Billy chucks crabapples down to them. He pauses to snap off a couple of the straight vertical branches, the sappers.

"Hey, Cal," Billy calls down. Callie ignores the old name. "What's the name of the Jogin's dog?"

"Ah, whattaya asking him for?" Kevin laughs. "Just because they're neighbors, Cal doesn't know any more about the giant than the rest of us."

Callie thinks about proving Kevin wrong, then decides anyone as willfully ignorant of what people want to be called as Kevin and Billy are don't deserve to know the dog's name.

Billy throws the sappers, one at a time, into the Jogin's yard, trying to get the dog to play fetch. When the dog doesn't rise to the occasion, Billy switches to the crapapples. The dog yelps with each near-hit.

"Having an off-day, pitcher?" Callie jokes, to draw Billy's attention from the dog before he hurts it. Billy twists in the tree and winds up. Two of the apples he launches at her do peg Callie, hard little things unforgiving against her bony shoulder and hip. But she doesn't complain. She knows what Billy wants, probably Kevin too—to establish their dominance. Today she doesn't feel like giving them the satisfaction of wincing or crying. She locks it up, turns around and scoops the apples off the ground.

She lobs them back at Billy, knowing she wouldn't hit him even if she was really trying. She smiles just enough to look like she's in on the joke but not so much that Billy would feel like Callie was fighting back. That's how you dealt with bullies effectively: let them think you'll take their abuse as part of their game, and they'll lay off the heavy-duty beat-downs they put on the other kids.

It's all fine until Kevin discovers the broken lock on Callie's father's storage shed. Busy half-heartedly tossing apples at Billy in the tree, Callie doesn't see Kevin go into the shed. She only becomes aware of what the other boy is up to when Kevin emerges from the shed, shaking cans of wasp spray and gear lubricant.

The sound brings Billy out of the tree with a solid "thwump," and a thick lower branch, perhaps weakened from age, perhaps not, crashes down under him. The bigger boy lands hard and grimaces as he loses his balance. He probably landed wrong on his ankle, Callie thinks, but he won't show any weakness. Callie stills her face, no indication that she'd seen the grimace or that she knows she could have jumped from higher in the tree and landed without rolling an ankle. No indication at how the sight of the downed branch, or the moist sappy spot where moments ago it still connected to the tree's trunk, makes her heart ache.

She knows every branch of this tree, her favorite from when she was a babe. At his first birthday, the story goes, Cal's uncle had carried him around the yard, pointing to different plants and naming them. Cal coo'ed and ahh'ed as babies do, until they reached the tree in the corner of the yard. The uncle told him it was a crabapple tree, and baby Cal laughed, reached out, wrapped his arms around the nearest branch and said something that sounded to everyone at the party like "MINE!" Cal cried when his uncle walked him away from the tree and crawled back to lay on the tree's roots four times that afternoon.

Callie stands frozen as the two bigger boys talk quietly, passing the metal aerosol cans between them. Before Callie can even react, Kevin paints a nonsensical pattern with the lubricant across the side of the shed and into the shrubs next to it. Billy arches a thumb at the fence that separates Callie's yard from the Jogin's.

Billy produces a cigarette lighter.

"Awesome," Kevin grunts.

Billy depresses the nozzle on the aerosol can, flicks the strikewheel on the lighter. A breath of flame shoots from the nozzle, and Billy advances on the crabapple tree, waving the makeshift flamethrower left and right. Some of the dryer, lower leaves spark.

Callie's blood boils. It doesn't matter what the plan was—burn the tree or something in the shed or launch a flaming projectile at the Jogin's dog—it would not stand. She would not let them do the same damage to her own property, or the Jogin's, that they were known to do to every public space in town.

"No!" Callie shouts. "Put the cans down, and get the hell off of my property."

"Little boy's got spunk," Billy laughs, turning back to the apple tree with the aerosol can in one hand, finger still on the nozzle, flame now licking the bark. "Like to see you stop me, Cal. Or try."

Callie makes a move towards Billy, knowing she'll just end up knocked on her ass or with a faceful of flame to scare her backwards. Kevin grabs her from behind, hauling hard on Callie's right elbow. Callie yelps in pain. Billy smiles.

"You know better, man," Kevin laughs. "You can't stop him."

"BUT I CAN," a deep voice rumbles from the other side of the fence. Billy pulls up short, yanking his finger away from the nozzle of the aerosol can and quickly dropping the still-hot lighter into his pocket. Callie takes small satisfaction in the look of discomfort on Billy's face, the only indication the hot metal of the rim or the striker has reached through Billy's pocket. Callie hopes there's a nice red mark on Billy's leg, not that she'll ever see it. Billy is not a boy whose pants she wants to get into.

The Jogin's head, shoulders and upper torso appear above the top of the wooden fence. Callie hadn't even sensed the portal to the Hidden Lands opening this time; unusual for her and a sure sign her anger is getting the better of her.

"We didn't know you were home, sir," Billy responds, his voice less confident.

"THAT SHOULDN'T MATTER, BILLY TAUGENT. RIGHT IS RIGHT. THAT PROPERTY IS NOT YOURS TO DESTROY."

"Yes, sir," Billy mutters.

Kevin releases Callie's arm and starts to inch towards the walkway out of Callie's yard.

"I SEE YOU AS WELL, KEVIN COLLUCI. YOU WILL BOTH APOLOGIZE TO CAL AND LEAVE NOW. DO NOT COME BACK. AND DO NOT THINK ABOUT CAUSING PROBLEMS LATER."

"Sorry, man," Kevin says without looking at Callie, head bowed and slouching towards the walkway along the house to the street. Billy doesn't even say that much, just pulls the lighter out of his pocket and absentmindedly flicks it to life as he follows Kevin.

Callie watches them go, knowing without looking that the Jogin is watching her and not them. When they reach the bottom steps of the walk, she rounds on the giant.

"That's it?" Callie barks, tears filling her eyes. "Go away, don't bother Callie again? No punishment? They were going to burn down my tree, Jogin! My tree! And probably hurt your dog, too!"

"CAL . . ."

"Callie!" And now the tears do burst. "You, of all people, should be calling me what I want to be called, not the name they gave me!"

Before she knows what she's doing, Callie has snatched the large downed branch Billy had broken earlier. The thinner end is in her hand, and the thicker end drags behind her, just reaching the ground and heavy enough to scratch a small trail through the grass. She's running on pure emotion. This level of anger usually only outwardly manifests when she's alone. She tries always to be the good boy, the quiet one who sits on the edge of the playground reading comic books or scratching pictures into the loose soil where the grass has died. But today . . .

"CALLIE, DON'T . . .," the Jogin calls, but she is beyond hearing him. Callie is tired of the platitudes, of being told she'll come into her own, tired of being told she needs to keep her head down and stay calm and not let anger get the best of her and educate through her actions and words. Despite what the Jogin might think, and Callie honestly can't tell what the giant is thinking in this moment, this anger is not about her identity. It's about Billy and Kevin damaging Callie's haven, her tree that she climbs up and reads in and peers into the Hidden Lands from. It's about Billy and Kevin being willing to injure the Jogin's dog, and not being afraid of the repurcussions because for them there never are any. They are just boys being boys. So she shuts the giant's words out and runs out of the backyard.

As Callie rushes down the walkway along the side of the house, the heavier end of the branch bounces on the gray cement unevenly laid by her father when Callie was still a baby. The branch beats out a rhythmless meter. It makes her feel stronger, helps her channel the anger.

By the time Callie clears the front steps of the house, Billy and Kevin are two houses down the hill and headed for the lake. She leaps the bottom three steps, lands in the center of the street in a crouch, and snarls.

It's not a loud snarl, but the sound carries, somehow, over the usual afternoon small community sounds of kids laughing on another street, someone mowing a lawn in the distance, cicadas chirring. Billy and Kevin turn, their posture indicating that they're not sure what they heard, what caught their attention. Callie rises out of her crouch, scrapes the branch along the blacktop so it rests in front of her.

"Dude," Kevin barks at the same time Billy laughs, "Are you serious? Goody little Calvin is finally standing up for himself?"

"You tried to burn down my tree," Callie responds. "I AM serious, Billy. I'm sick of you two getting away with shit like this. All you do is wreck stuff."

"A talent for destruction is still a talent," Billy mocks with a smirk on his face. Kevin's eyebrows quirk as if to ask, Who the hell are you quoting?

"Don't come near my house again," Callie shouts. "And don't come near me."

"Or what, baby boy?" Billy's voice grows hard; he takes three steps uphill towards Callie. Kevin looks unsure of how to react: assist or back away.

"Come and find out," Callie answers. She hefts the

branch so the heavier end leaves the ground. The cords in her right arm pop, and her hand tightens around the lighter end of the branch, drawing the whole thing up and back.

"Billy. Let's just go. He's not worth it." Kevin reaches for his friend's shoulder, casting a wary eye towards the Jogin's house even though he knows the Jogin cannot leave his own property. His fingers touch Billy's shirt, but the bigger boy just shrugs him off, advancing up the street. "Cal," Kevin starts to plead, "Dude, back down, so we can all walk away."

"No," Callie shakes her head. "Not this time. I'm tired of walking away. Billy burned my tree. Almost hurt the Jogin's dog. The Jogin won't . . . can't . . . do anything because you're not on his property threatening the Boundary to the Hidden Lands. I can do something, and it's time I did."

"Yeah," Billy agrees, and a disturbing leer appears on his face. "You can get the crap beaten out of you." He breaks into a run, shoulders hunched forward, fingers clenched into fists.

Callie plants her feet, brings the branch up like a bat. Adrenalin pumping, it doesn't feel as heavy as it should. Muscle memory from Little League bubbles up, and she imagines Billy's head as a steady slowball pitch high and center. Her mind lines up the shot. Billy doesn't slow despite the branch's clear positioning.

"Faggot nancy boy," Billy blurts, obviously hoping his words will distract Callie. They don't.

She swings with precision, bringing the branch down like a golf club (more muscle memory, from outings with that same nature-loving uncle) instead of out straight like a bat. Billy has one second to sneer at what he must think is a predictable failure of will before the branch—thicker than he'd realized, harder for how fresh and green it is—slams into his left leg just below the knee.

Callie hears the snap of bone, feels it through the shudder of the branch, followed by Billy's surprised grunt as his momentum carries him into her. She didn't expect to come out of this unscathed, of course. As he hits, she relaxes her braced legs and falls with his impact. There's no time to roll; the best she can do is keep the back of her head from slamming into the road. Her ass hits the ground first, then her shoulder-blades. Her legs start to launch into the air, but she manages to bring them back down.

Billy's scream only starts when his injured leg hits pavement. It doesn't start low, the way Callie has seen it play out in the movies. One second Billy is grunting from the bat's impact, and the next he is keening, a high-pitched sound Callie can only associate with banshees. Billy rolls off of her, clutching his leg, landing on the branch and keening more. Callie jumps to her feet, weaponless but ready to defend against the follow-up attack she expects from Kevin.

But Kevin is still halfway down the street, and his posture suggests he is not about to charge. He looks angry but unsure of what to do about it.

"Get away from him, you little bitch," he calls. "I don't want any more trouble. Just leave so I can help Billy get home. If he can walk, that is."

"First gender reference you've gotten right all day, Kevin," she answers.

"Is that what this was about?" he shouts back.

"No. It's about my tree. And the Jogin's dog. And all the other property you guys have wrecked this summer. Someone has to protect this side, the human side of the Boundary, since the Jogin can only protect the Boundary itself. Because you two, and other kids like you, will just keep screwing with everything you don't like or don't need until someone stands up to you."

"You mean screwing with people like you."

"Billy doesn't like me." Callie pauses, looks down at the still-moaning bigger boy. "I thought you used to, when we were little. Maybe you never did. Either way, you don't need me now."

"Cal . . ."

"It's over, Kevin. Get Billy help. I tried not to hit too hard, but he'll still need a cast. Don't come back to my house, even if your parents come to dinner like usual. Don't come near me when school starts again. And don't . . . don't think about revenge." She looks down again. "You hear that, Billy? This is over. New era. You spread the word: I'm the new human protector of this town."

"That's just a legend," Kevin starts, but Callie's look cuts him off.

"Doesn't matter," she nods. "It's real as of now."

Callie stoops down close to Billy. He's no longer moaning. She reaches under him and grabs the end of her branch. Billy's eyes lock with hers, an unspoken easy way or hard moment between them, and then Billy eases himself up enough for the branch to slide free. It looks for a moment like he's going to grab the other end as it passes his chest, but he doesn't move. Callie hefts the branch over her shoulder, nods once more at Kevin, and turns her back on the boys.

Doors shut quickly on several of the houses up the road. People were watching. People heard. Word will spread quicker than if she had to rely on Billy and Kevin alone. She'll face challenges—Billy's parents will likely pursue legal action for injuring their boy—and that's okay too.

Callie keeps her posture erect, her face schooled to stillness, until she's in her back yard and out of sight of everyone. Everyone except the Jogin, who is leaning on the fence between their yards, or at least leaning as much of his weight as the fence will hold.

"You knew." She exhales. A light dances into her eyes. "You've known all along and you never said anything!"

The giant shrugs as if it doesn't matter. "THE HIDDEN LANDS CREATE. THEY DESTROY. YOU HAD TO COME TO IT IN YOUR OWN TIME, CALLIE, AND FOR THE RIGHT REASONS. YOU ARE THE BALANCE BETWEEN MY WORLD," he pauses, nodding at the portal to the Hidden Lands and then again at the street, "AND THEIRS."

Callie drags the branch off of her shoulder. It's heavy again, the way it was when she picked it up. Being a protector, speaking up for that part of the world that can't speak for itself . . . she feels a moment of trepidation.

"What if you're wrong?"

"IT IS NOT MY DECISION. THERE ARE NO CHOSEN ONES, ONLY THOSE WHO THEMSELVES MAKE A CHOICE."

"My parents are going to freak out."

Anthony R. Cardno calls northwest New Jersey home when he's not traveling the country as an instructor on regulatory compliance. His short fiction has appeared or is forthcoming in *Shroud, Willard & Maple, Chelsea*

Station, Beyond the Sun, Oomph (A Little Super Goes A Long Way), Tales of the Shadowmen, Vol. 1, Full Throttle Space Tales Vol 6, and *Galactic Games.* He edited the charity anthology *The Many Tortures of Anthony Cardno,* with work by twenty-two genre authors, and wrote a short Christmas novel, *The Firflake.* He can usually be found on Twitter as @talekyn and on anthonycardno.com.

TESTING, TESTING, 1-2-3

Susan Bianculli

Deanna jolted upright in her darkened bedroom with a gasp, her blue eyes wide as she clutched the white bed sheets to her chest. The alarms of her nightmare merged with the alarm ringing in her ears, and for a moment she couldn't separate the two. She looked around the room, befuddled with both sleep and panic. It took a moment for her brain to register the Farm-wide emergency klaxon. But was it real, or just a drill?

When the extra-terrestrial colony had been established, everyone, no matter their age, had been given an Emergency Duty Station for any Farm drill or crisis that happened. Deanna's parents, Elizabeth and Amory, had been assigned to EDS #2, the Science section's chemistry labs. Deanna, being fifteen years old, had ended up being assigned not with her parents, but to EDS #12. That was the unit responsible for securing the Dining Hall and the Kitchen—two areas important for the overall well-being of the colonists, if not as technologically important to the colony's scientific infrastructure.

Deanna shoved her short blonde hair out of her eyes as she struggled up out of the twisted-up sheets of the bed and punched her window's computer screen on. It lit up to show a calm, pre-dawn picture of mist drifting across early spring grass, which was at odds with the electronic wails of the corridor's siren. The clock in the lower right corner said it was only 5:31 AM.

Spaceflot! This can't be just a drill, then—it's too early! she thought as she looked at the little blinking numbers.

All of a sudden, through the door of her tiny bedroom she heard the running feet of her parents. They called out to her to get moving as they dashed out of the family cubicle into the main hallway towards their assignments. That galvanized her almost as much as the sirens did. Deanna hopped onto the carpeted floor and ran to her bureau by the window screen's dim light. She wrenched its plastic drawers open and pulled out the first thing that came to hand, a green-and-brown jumpsuit. She yanked it onto her body as fast as she could slither out of her pajamas, tossing the purple rayon material that she'd worn to sleep in onto the floor and stuffing her feet into the sturdy rubber shoes that were always beside her closet. She bolted out her bedroom door before the clock reached 5:34 AM.

Deanna made it to the colony's Dining Hall in a record three and a half minutes later, according to the chronometer imprinted on her jumpsuit's cuff. Her rubber soles squeaked on the grey and white linoleum tiled floor as she barreled into the cavernous room. The black metal tables and benches of the room eerily reflected the red emergency lights in the ceiling, which also glinted off the glass southern wall, its windows, and its outside access door. Deanna, as she rounded a table, was horrified to be able to see the tilled fields in the growing light beyond the clear wall. The defensive shields hadn't been lowered! She ran to the control box in the corner where the transparent wall and the plascrete wall met up. Worryingly, in the background almost over and above the siren's racket, were abnormal sounds of banging coming from the Kitchen.

What are the others doing in there? The windows are supposed to be the first thing to be taken care of in an emergency! she thought in concern and annoyance. She slapped at the controls that would lower the protective metal.

"Come on, come on!" she said to the reinforced wall, repeatedly smacking one fist into the palm of her other hand in impatience as the metal moved too ponderously downward for her liking.

As the shield neared the top of the glass door that led to the outside, Deanna caught a flash of red and brown movement bolting towards her across the grass. She blinked—that was Rebecca! What was her best friend doing out there, when she should be in here helping with the emergency? Realizing that Rebecca would never make it before the metal closed off the door, Deanna slammed her hands down on the control panel and accidentally hit the 'stop' and 'reverse' touch-pads at the same time. The mechanism faltered, groaning and shuddering as it tried to obey both commands. The teen swore as her friend reached the entrance and tried to pry it open, but the shield had already passed below the top of the outward swinging door.

"Hang on, Rebecca!" Deanna cried to her through the glass, and she banged one hand down on just the reverse pad this time.

The metal wall resolved its difficulties and started going up, freeing the entrance. The brown-haired girl slipped inside, and Deanna mashed the 'down' pad again.

"Thanks!" gasped Rebecca as she doubled over breathing hard, her hair falling down over her face.

The shield-wall thunked into its groove in the floor behind them.

"What the hell were you doing out there?" Deanna practically shouted at her.

"I couldn't sleep, so I'd gone for an early morning

walk to look at the wheat fields and watch the sun rise! How was I supposed to know there'd be an emergency?" Rebecca half-shouted back. She took a big breath and straightened up, tucking her long hair behind her ears. "Do—do we know what's going on yet? What's happening in the kitchen?"

Rebecca's questions jolted Deanna. There was still too much noise coming from the kitchen, and Deanna hadn't seen anybody else yet from their EDS station. Just then several screams, followed by an explosion and a loud whooshing hiss, caused both teens to jump.

"I dunno, but we're going to find out! Come on!" Deanna said, grabbing for Rebecca's hand to yank her along behind.

Hand-in-hand the two girls ran to the opposite side of the dining hall to open the door that led into the food prep area. Both coughed as they got an unexpected faceful of smoke when it swung open. Remembering their fire training, they crouched down and covered their mouths and noses with the crook of their arms as they peered in. Inside the huge, stainless steel industrial kitchen, the food preparation area had exploded in chaos. Twisted blackened hunks of metal that once were parts of stoves lay scattered about, water gushed out of broken pipes, food dispensers spewed ingredients all over the counters and floors, and one oven still partially attached to the wall had flames spouting out of it. A loud electronic sound came out of the speakers in the kitchen that sounded eerily like laughter.

"What's happening?! Has the computer gone mad?" Deanna shouted over the commotion, hoping someone could answer.

Across the room, the AI that normally assisted the colonists in making meals rotated its computerized camera/screen combination to face them. It was shorting out badly, sparks flying from the casing, and the jagged horizontal glitches in the screen made the usually calm and soothing androgynous face look twisted and demonic. The computer chef screeched incomprehensibly at the teens crouched in the doorway.

"Deanna! Rebecca!" Manny, one of the sub-cooks, pulled himself awkwardly along a counter top towards the two girls. "We received a new cooking program beamed from Earth last night, and we uploaded it to the kitchen mainframe this morning," he gasped out, his leg bent at an unnatural angle and his pant leg wet with blood. "It was supposed to up the proficiency of the AI, but instead . . .."

Rebecca shrieked, and Deanna looked over in time to see her friend duck out of the way of a wildly swinging, fiery gas line. Deanna ducked, too, but Manny wasn't as fast. It hit him in the face and knocked him unconscious to the floor. The AI laughed an electronically demented laugh.

"The new program must have scrambled its brain! Now

what do we do?" Rebecca yelled frantically to Deanna.

The two teens saw that the line which had missed hitting them was only one of many fuel lines that were knocking food, cooking utensils and pots and pans off every available surface, all orchestrated by the now madly cackling kitchen computer. To make it even worse, little gouts of flame at each hose tip spread fire as they came in contact with pooling flammable substances. It was a wonder the fires hadn't ignited inside the free-flying fuel lines yet. Amidst the wreckage, the girls saw several people on the ground writhing in pain, the jumpsuits melted from their bodies in places along with the flesh underneath, exposing horribly reddened and bubbled skin.

"Chemical burns!" shouted Rebecca over the noise.

Deanna pointed sharply to the right side of the room. "That must be from the stove banks—the mixed gas mains have exploded! We gotta grab people and get them out into the dining . . . oh, god, no—the shields are down! Quick, Rebecca! Go raise the perma-steel wall so we can open the windows and door to get fresh air in here before we are gassed to death!" yelled Deanna.

The kitchen computer screamed in denial when Rebecca grabbed Manny up from where he'd fallen. She struggled only a little to half-drag him out of the kitchen and lay him on the floor just outside the door. Behind her, Deanna helped a stout woman from Stores named Sveda to her feet and out to the nearest dining room bench while managing to avoid yet another flailing line. As Rebecca left them all at a run and wove a path between the tables to do as Deanna had said, Deanna took a deep breath and held it as she dived back into the kitchen.

"S-stop! T-turn it all off b-before you do anything else!" gasped a bloodied woman half-lying not far away on the floor.

It was Bethe, the head of Deanna's emergency group and the person whose orders she was supposed to follow. Bethe choked, pointed weakly in the direction of the other end of the kitchen, and then slumped all the way to the floor, unconscious.

"You will not, Human!" screamed the computer, just self-aware enough to perceive the threat to itself.

Grimacing but still holding her breath, Deanna dodged her way across the kitchen floor, steering clear of the thrashing lines and fires now being aimed at her and praying for no more explosions to happen while people were still in the area. She avoided the messes of nameless food substances on the floor, but as she jumped a large spreading milk puddle, a hose smacked her on the top of her head from behind. Deanna saw stars and fell to all fours on landing, a bleeding lump already rising in her hair.

The AI cackled in triumph.

Deanna nearly gasped with the pain, but she managed to remember to keep hold of her breath as she scrambled to her feet. She darted looks around her as she dodged three more hoses intent on doing her more bodily harm, searching for the kitchen shut-off switch. She saw with relief that the red plastic emergency panel, which controlled all electricity to the kitchen, was on the wall not far away. Deanna flung herself at it.

"Noooooo!" the computer screamed as it sent all its flexible hoses after her, but its own glitching, having grown worse even since Deanna had entered the kitchen, kept the computer from accurately aiming any at her.

Deanna pounded out the emergency override sequence on the touch-pad, but nothing happened. She felt a growing need to breathe and looked at it frantically to figure out why it wasn't working. She then saw the small lit symbol on the screen which indicated that the pad was locked. She slammed the opposite symbol to unlock it and punched the code in again. The AI wailed inarticulately at her, all the hoses in the kitchen going even madder than they had been before, but this time Deanna was successful. The electricity powered down instantly.

In the sudden near-darkness of the kitchen, the waving tentacle-like lines all around her fell limply like harpooned octopi, the flames dying in their hoses as the gases slowed to a stop. Even the blazing stove went out.

Deanna, in need of air, forgot herself and sighed in relief. She choked on the fouled air that she took in and realized her mistake as everything went dark.

Machine clicks and whirrs filled an otherwise empty central control room with soft sounds. A section on one of the many burnished metal panels glowed to life and shot two different beams of light at two separate receptors on the wall across the room. Hidden wall panels slid aside as two life-like ambulatory robots dressed in white lab coats exited from the compartments. They left the room with a measured tread and headed down the metal corridor towards Testing Lab Two. Opening the door, they crossed the white, sterile environment to where Colonist 836-143, otherwise known as Deanna when awake, lay asleep on the gurney that the androids had brought her in on from her suspended animation pod a couple of hours ago. The life-like robots removed the white sheet that had been covering the teen for warmth and went to work releasing her from the leads that connected her brain to the Emergency Preparedness Routine's virtual environment simulator.

"Return Colonist 836-143 to her pod. Begin sanitization procedure for Testing Lab Two. Ready Colonist 836-144 for Testing Lab Three," was the monotone transmission they received in their earpieces when they were finished freeing her.

The androids beeped, acknowledging the command, and wheeled the still sleeping Deanna out, pausing only long enough to activate the sensor that would start the room's sterilization process. The robots took her down the corridors of the hushed starship towards the cold storage bays, passing other sleeping colonists on other gurneys being wheeled by androids to their various destinations. The deep space vessel Trans-dimensional Mage was still some years out from its destination of Kepler-438b in the constellation of Lyra, but it was the duty of the colony ship's central AI to make sure that every one of the colonists, who were all making the trip via cold sleep, had the best chance of survival upon arrival. And that meant testing and re-testing by virtual reality the crisis knowledge and reactions of the people who were going to make the far away Earth-like planet, the first one ever discovered by humans way back in January of 2015, their new home.

The androids stopped Deanna's gurney in front of her suspended animation unit and carefully lifted her back inside, rearranging her limbs so she would lie in the most comfortable position on the water-foam padding. She was then re-connected to her pod's myriad lifelines and monitors, with everything being tested to assure they were in perfect working order after the final lead was in place. Lastly, she was re-connected by her special brain port to the control panel and the built-in teaching unit of the pod before the transparent lid was closed. Once the life-extending cold mist was registered to be seeping properly into the suspended animation unit once more, the androids left to carry out the rest of their orders.

The ship's central AI, upon receiving the update that the subject assessed in Testing Lab Two was now re-situated in her pod, noted the test results in the appropriate file: *Colonist 836-143—Failed Kitchen EPR test 3/6/2305; did not wait until clear of poisonous vapors, known to be present, to breathe. Next scheduled test: 3/6/2306.*

As the androids' footfalls faded away down the corridor, inside her pod an unknowing Deanna grimaced slightly as she dreamed about sitting down at her personal computer to log in to another boring lecture about Kitchen safety procedures.

Susan Bianculli wears the titles "Mother" and "Wife" most proudly. Another is "Author" for her *The Mist Gate Crossings* series, as well as several short stories in several other anthologies besides this one. To learn about the other things she's had published, check out: susanbianculli.wix.com/home

EIGHTEEN ROSES

Ameria Lewis

It was a beautiful day. Liza's favorite kind of day: blue sky, a few puffy white clouds, and a bit of a breeze. She would be waiting, Calla knew, where she always waited: on the bench overlooking the ornamental pond. She would be watching the koi as they swam among the water greenery and smiling at the tinkling music of the little waterfall.

Calla half-skipped down the walk, eager to see Liza's face again and to tell her all the news from the past year. Who was seeing who, what'd happened when Challenger 20 had landed on Rigel, which college had accepted her, and most importantly how Liza's parents were doing. There was so much to tell and so little time to do it!

Calla rounded a bend, and there she was: just a little bit different from last year. Was her hair darker, her face thinner, and was she just a bit taller? It was harder for

Calla to remember each year, but Liza's eyes were as blue as the sky above, as always, and she still looked like Liza. Bright, independent, brave Liza.

Calla waved as Liza turned away from the koi pond and saw her. Liza's familiar grin answered, and the two girls raced across the green grass to throw their arms around each other, laughing as they spun around and around until they were dizzy.

"I haven't done that in ages!" Calla gasped.

"Liar," Liza retorted cheerfully. "It's been exactly one year, almost to the minute."

"Sooooo literal," Calla drawled.

"When I want to be," Liza nodded. "Now, catch me up on everything!"

Two hours sped by before Calla knew it. They spoke of old friends and Calla's new boyfriend. Calla shared the news of her college acceptance, and then they talked about Liza's parents and family. Liza laughed when Calla told her about Liza's brother's recent antics that drove her grandmother to yelling dire threats if he didn't behave. As their time neared an end, the light dimmed then brightened again. Calla reluctantly stood up and brushed the grass from her jeans. "I have to go," she said sadly.

"I know," Liza nodded. "I'll see you next year. You can tell me all about college. Bring your sketchbook; I want to see what you're designing."

"I will," Calla agreed as she reached out to hug her friend. "Why does your grandmother call you ladybug?"

Liza grinned. "She always did, ever since I was a baby. I don't know why."

Calla looked over her shoulder several times as she walked slowly up the path to the exit. Liza watched her go, but her friend's expression didn't hold the same sorrow that was in Calla's heart. It couldn't. Liza didn't know the truth. Calla could leave the virtual reality suite, but Liza never could.

Jeff read the card again and shook his head. His boss was a weird guy. Most places used auto-delivery, but Harrison insisted that flower deliveries required the human touch. Jeff didn't get it, but it was nice to see how people reacted to getting flowers. He'd made deliveries to all sorts of places, but this was the first time he'd delivered to the VR Café, although not the first time he'd had to make a delivery at a specific time. It was the first time that he'd had to call someone else to find out what that time would be.

The hall was lined with doors, some of which glowed a faint red to indicate they were occupied. Others were green, with rate charts neatly illuminated on them. Jeff had never been in a VR suite, and at those rates he never would, unless he was proposing or something.

A girl was just coming out of the suite he'd been told to find. "Calla Sanderson?"

"Yes?" She turned around and smiled at him, but her eyes were shiny in that way girls' eyes were before they started crying. No way was he sticking around for the waterworks.

"These are for you," he said quickly, handing her the flowers. "Eighteen pink roses. Happy birthday!"

"But it's not my bir—" Jeff was out of earshot before she finished her sentence.

Calla looked at the dozen and a half pink roses framed by dark, glossy green leaves and accented with white baby's breath. It wasn't her birthday. It was Liza's. Who would have sent her Liza's birthday flowers? Who would have sent Liza birthday flowers?

"Read the card, goose," Calla murmured, opening the envelope holding the vidcard.

After a second's hesitation, the recording started playing. Calla's breath caught sharply in her throat as Liza's fourteen year old face grinned back at her.

"So," Liza said, "you know that dream I had, the bad one, which led to us making promises to each other? I started thinking about it again, and, Calla, I know you. I know you'll be here, and I know what you'll be doing. If you're receiving these roses, that means my dream wasn't as silly as we pretended. What teenager dreams about dying and believes it will happen? Just me!"

On the vidcard, Liza's smile faded. "You're my best friend. You're better than a sister. I don't know how many years you've been coming, but you don't need to come anymore. It's not really me in that recording, and it's not fair to ask you to keep doing this. Remember me in your heart, Calla, but not this way. Remember I love you, and that will be enough."

The memory on the vidcard ran out, but Calla couldn't see it anymore. Her tears blurred everything. She blinked her vision clear and saw a little ladybug with red and black wings crawling on one of the leaves. She smiled, remembering Liza's grandmother calling her ladybug.

"All right, Liza," she whispered. "I'll always remember you, I promise."

The ladybug's wings flared open and it took flight—first brushing the tip of her nose before flitting out of sight.

Ameria Lewis lived the life of an American gypsy for most of her adult life, floating from state to state as the whim and wish took her. Ameria has run a writing club for nearly 20 years, attends college as a non-traditional student, and won NaNoWriMo for the first time in 2013. She is currently pausing in northwest Louisiana, for who knows how long.

ALIEN TRUCE

Nori Odoi

The red sun glinted off the polished emerald skin of the Tektris representative. Seven feet tall, ruler straight and just as thin, his many appendages swayed in the light breeze. The eyes were large, multifaceted orbs and instead of lips, pedipalps moved constantly. The creature smelled of flowers and spice. Despite her fear, Maya found it intriguing and oddly beautiful.

"Those damn Mantises," her father Palant muttered, clenching his fist on the arm of his wheelchair. "We're at their mercy, and they know it."

The fighting between Magellan Colony and the Tektris was only a few months old. For twenty years, the colony had flourished on Tahiti. It was settled on the northern continent with its balmy climate and fertile soil, avoiding the south with its dense jungles and wide swaths of desert. When the Colonial War broke out seventeen years ago, just after Maya was born, the settlers were almost relieved to lose contact with the contentious outer planets—no one wanted to go off world and fight someone else's battles. They were content to be on their own, self governing and self sufficient. Then a few months ago, they had met the Tektris, and the colony found itself in a war of its own.

The Tektris representative walked over to the two, looming over the crippled man and his daughter. Its eyes swiveled to examine each of them in turn. Then it pulled a bag of sewn purple and gold leaves forward. With another limb, it reached into the bag.

Maya felt Palant flinch almost imperceptibly—like her mother and the other settlers, he found all of the creatures of this world repulsive and sometimes terrifying. But Maya loved their intricate symmetry and vivid coloration. She spent her free hours watching the animals just beyond the settlement, studying them, finding their behavior so different from the Earth-imported animals. She never saw one attack another. There were confrontations, but not only did one always back down gracefully, but there were what seemed to be signs of affection afterwards.

She wished Janta was here. He shared her fascination with Tahiti's wildlife. They had met while watching two antelope-monkeys tussle—then make up with an amazing display of acrobatics. Even then, Maya found herself distracted by the way Janta's black hair twisted into mischievous tufts and the roughness of his hand when it brushed hers accidentally. Last night they had kissed on the crosswalk between the settlement houses, under the glow of Tahiti's three moons.

From the bag, the Tektris pulled a dull gray ball. It reached over gracefully and dropped it in Palant's lap. Palant picked it up and turned it around in his hands. He and Maya had seen this before.

After the last battle, when all was lost, and it seemed that the Tektris would break through and destroy the colony, the fighting had suddenly stopped. Balls like this were thrown all around the protecting walls of the settlement. The colonists thought they were explosives, but before they could destroy them, a wall of wailing sound poured out of them. Then silence. Then these words:

"We are Tektris Society. We will speak. Send your Society Speaker. We will not end him. If you do not, you will be ended."

A strange motion brought Maya back to the present. The Tektris was gesturing with one long, jointed appendage while using another limb to lift its ball to the level of its pedipalps.

"I speak here. You know there." The strange tinny voice came from the ball that Palant was holding. Maya noticed that the sound actually coming from the Tektris was more like a series of crackling noises. "You speak there. I know here."

"I am Palant," Maya's father said. "I am the leader of the colony. I have come to meet with you as you asked."

"I am Dkshp. What is this one?"

"This is Maya. She is my helper."

The Tektris began swaying. Its pedipalps began twitching back and forth, and a crackling noise could be heard. Maya realized that it was rubbing and tapping two of its limbs together in a jerky percussion. Something bright flashed. Just behind the Tektris, a round, furry creature was rolling about. It was a bright red with two long, green tufts, and it moved first to one side then the other.

"What is that?" Palant asked, following Maya's eyes.

"That is my zztt akk, my zddt dkk." Palant looked blank, and the Tektris kept trying. "That is my zbt, my dkd."

Dkshp reached out to the red creature. For a moment there was silence. "No. I know now. That is my helper. We did not know your Society had helpers. This is good."

Maya's breath tumbled out in a river of relief. Palant was the colony's leader; everyone agreed he was the one who needed to negotiate their surrender. But he was wheel-chair bound—crippled during one of the Tektris battles. He couldn't go alone. Maya had begged to accompany him, despite her mother's tearful protests. Maya had been helping Palant manage ever since he had been injured. She had a sixth sense about what he needed and when. She had accompanied him to all the colony's meetings, filed his papers, and even sat with him late at night as he outlined possible strategies for the colony's survival. She knew she could help him better than anyone else.

But she remembered Janta's whisper as they said goodbye, "Maya, stay here! The Tektris only asked for one speaker. We should not send two people." She had just turned away, knowing that she had to go.

Dkshp interrupted her thoughts, "We speak now. Your Society ended many Tektris. Tektris eating and drinking. Your Society came. You ended Tektris. "

"We did not know what you were. We were exploring, and we thought," Palant hesitated for a moment. "We, uhmm, didn't know you were people. That is, we thought you were, uhmm, animals. I mean, uhmmm, we'd never seen anything like you before."

"I do not know your speak."

"It's hard to explain, but we made a terrible mistake. We know that, and we are sorry."

Maya remembered when the men sent to explore the southern lands had returned with many strange specimens they had shot during their trip. People had tried to figure out if the corpses of what they now called Tektris could be used in some way—they were dissected and analyzed.

Their tough waterproof skins were made into hats and leather carry bags. The meat was analyzed and then fed to the pigs brought from Earth.

No one was prepared when the mutilated bodies of the next team of explorers were thrown before the walls of the colony. No one was prepared for the horror of farmers massacred in their fields and cut into bloody slabs. When the final attack came, the sheer number of Tektris drove the colonists back behind their walls, but they knew they could not fight them off long. They could not reach the outer worlds; they had no allies and limited supplies. Their only hope was to find a way to make peace.

She felt a soft caress on her ankle. The furry creature had come to her and was rubbing against her. She stretched out her hand, and what seemed to be the creature's nose touched her fingers very, very gently. The nose was moist and cool. Timidly she fingered the inviting fur. Her father was busy talking to the Tektris. He didn't need her for the moment.

She knelt down and stroked the tiny, round body, alert to any sign of displeasure on its part. Instead the creature began to vibrate gently, pulsing beneath her fingers, and causing waves of happiness to stream up her arm and then fill her whole body. The smell of cinnamon surrounded her. She forgot the desperate situation, forgot her heavy sense of responsibility. All of it washed away by a wave of affection for the creature beside her.

She listened to her father's voice, sometimes pleading, sometimes angry. He had clearly forgotten about her. She could relax for the moment.

Maya suddenly realized that her legs were very tired, and the ground looked so soft. She sat down and leaned against the boulder behind her. The round creature rolled into her lap. As she looked at it, she realized that beneath each of the two green tufts there was a large black eye gazing liquidly into hers. When she rubbed the fur behind the eyes, they half closed in pleasure, and the vibrating continued. The fur seemed softer than any fabric she had ever felt, almost melting between her fingers.

The nights of tossing and turning on her small bed began to catch up with her, and she dozed. She dreamed of life on the small settlement, of the hard work of farming and the joyful gatherings for harvest and celebration. She saw the twinkle in her mother's eye and the slow smile of approval her father gave when she did everything right. Sleepily she remembered the alien animals playing on the edges of the settlement and the dancing in her heart when she heard Janta's quick step. She loved this world with its violet skies and magenta grasses; she could never understand her mother's yearning for yellow suns, blue skies, and single moons.

Images of the Tektris came into her mind, so stately

and tall, so amusingly limbed. If only the colonists had known they were intelligent, maybe they could have been friends. How amazing to see this world from such a different point of view. And this little furry creature, perhaps she could have come to know it too—learn what it had to teach. Too late. Too late. Too late.

She awoke with a start, one hand on the ground, one hand still buried in fur softer than clouds. The dark eyes were looking at her, but she sensed a restlessness, and she set it free. It skittered across the ground, ricocheting off Dkshp, and began to hum softly. The Tektris stopped speaking and drew itself up to its full height.

"Enough," it said loudly.

Maya scrambled to her feet and walked to her father's side, the terror awakened once more.

"I haven't finished," Palant said. "You haven't let me finish."

"The speak is done." Dkshp said. "The Societies know what will be."

"You can't decide. You don't understand yet."

"I do not make what will be. That is not my job. My job is to speak."

"Then who decides. Let me speak to him."

"The one who makes what will be does not speak. The one who speaks does not make what will be."

"You tricked us then! This has all been a waste of time."

Dkshp began to shake his limbs in an agitated way again, his pedipalps moving asynchronously. His helper rolled around him, and Dkshp reached out and touched it for a moment. He calmed down immediately.

"You do not know. I do not know why you do not know. We spoke. That was needed. But the helpers know what will be. We are only speakers. Your helper and my helper have pzzzt zzzt. Together they have made what will be.

"Your helper has shown your Society is not the Societies. You do not know us. We do not know you. But your new ones begin to know us."

"From this time, your Society is in this place. Only in this place. If you go to other places, you will be ended. But my helper will be with your helper. They will know each other. Your other new ones will also know. When your Society is ready, the Societies will come to speak and to be. Then we will see what will happen."

Palant was silent for a moment, trying to understand what all this meant. If nothing else, it meant the colony might survive. He reached out and took Maya's hand. "My helper would be happy to work with your helper. We will be happy to learn of the Societies."

"Yes!" Maya said. She tried to remember Dkshp's words. "We will know each other. Our Societies will know each other." She stretched her finger towards the red creature, and it came to her. As she touched its fur, new feelings surged through her—hope, reassurance, the knowledge that things can change and still be good. This world at last would truly be her home. Hers and Janta's.

Nori Odoi is a writer and poet who has been published in the *Old Farmers Almanac*, *The Anthology of New England Writers*, and *With Love, Lotus*. Though she prefers short fiction, she is currently working on her first novel about grief and loss and, of course, cats.

TERROR

Walt Socha

Daniel dropped his bookbag on the desk, scattering his models of fighting machines, and collapsed on his bed. Why couldn't they just leave him alone? His stomach roiled at the image of Cody's gloating face as Daniel scurried over the hallway floor, grabbing for his books. It had sucked enough being surrounded by Cody's hoard of friends, but Priscilla had been watching from down the hallway.

If only he could show those bullies. He'd kung fu them. No, he'd pull out a sword and whack off hunks of their greasy hair as they stood trembling. Priscilla would smile at him.

He lay back on the bed, willing his heaving gut to settle, staring at the models of flying machines hanging from the ceiling. He could still smell the stink of Cody's breath as the jerk laughed.

As he let out a long breath, his head exploded . . .

Dan, you okay?" The voice was far away. A girl's voice. Strange accent.

The pain lessened. Cold metal pushed up at his hands. Girl? Metal? An acrid smell stung his nose. Fire? His parents. He had to warn them. He opened his eyes. Dim lights. Metal walls. Low ceiling of pipes and wires.

He sat up. Then braced himself on the metal grillwork of the floor as a wave of pain and nausea swept through his body.

"By Mechan, that's a gash." A face appeared. "You really banged your head."

"What happened?" Daniel tried to stand. Swayed. Something hard brushed his shoulder.

"Wrap your head with this." A body formed under the face, and a hand held a soiled rag. "And let's go. We gotta get the transfer case oiled, or Sarge will lash us."

Transfer case? Daniel looked at the metal girders, narrow passages, crisscrossing beams and pipes so low he couldn't stand up straight. He was in the lower maintenance level of a land corvette. Four massive legs, three inch plate armor, quad diesel engines and dual two inch cannons. He'd oiled, replaced filters, and cleaned every interior surface of the walking war beast.

He froze. How did he know all that? He looked at the girl. Prisca. One of the oil rats in this military fighting machine. She was the only friend he'd ever known, a child small enough to scamper through the tight maintenance passageways, a slave held bound by a shock collar.

"Yeah, let's go." He couldn't think now. He wound the rag around his head and tucked the free end under his own collar. "I'll be okay." He stepped into the access tunnel.

As they slipped into the next cavity, the structure shuttered.

"By Mechan, we're getting ready to walk." Prisca moved to the right of a massive mechanical assembly, ducking under pipes and cables. "Let's get these gears oiled up. Shells'll be flying soon."

Daniel took the left side. Unscrewed a fill cap and peered at the attached rod. Low. He reached behind and grabbed a can from a rack. He popped the can and poured the viscous fluid into the tube. Totally unfamiliar. Yet he knew every move. Had to be a dream. But the metal was hard, the smells biting.

"You rats slacking?" A low-pitched voice cut through the whirl of shafts and the grinding of gears.

Sarge's face squeezed into the chamber. Ice formed in Daniel's gut as those squinting eyes looked around.

"Almost done, Sir." Daniel averted his eyes, moving to the next oil stick. Sarge whipped slaves who stared.

"Right side done, Sir." Prisca's voice cut through the din.

"Get up to the bay. Supplies to stow." The face retreated.

As they crawled out of an access shaft, they found the

bay doors still open. Through the opening, they could see the back end of a supply transport receding on six ponderous legs, crushing its way one step at a time through the forest to the safety of the rear lines.

Several supply boxes and two ammunition cases filled the only only space in the land corvette.

Sarge entered through the main hatch and pointed to the boxes. "Get the food stowed."

He turned as two corvette gunners entered the bay. Sarge bit his lip and stared as the two soldiers picked up one of the heavy ammunition cases and, grunting, sidled through the hatch towards the forward guns.

Once they disappeared, Sarge moved to the opening and reached for the bay door controls. Then jerked at an explosion of sound. He spun around, eyes wide.

Prisca stood frozen over a broken box of food cans. Several punctured cans oozed a brownish liquid at her feet. Others rolled over the metal mesh flooring.

"Maybe it's time to retire you," bellowed Sarge, his face a livid red.

Daniel froze. Retire? When child slaves got too big to move easily through the walking machine's maintenance shafts, they were sent to the mines to die. If they were lucky. Some of the girls were sent to the R and R camps. Rumors hinted that was even worse than the mines.

Sarge pulled out his lash as he moved towards Prisca.

His massive hand enveloped the handle containing the batteries that allowed the thin metal whips to fry nerves as well as cut flesh.

Blood pounded through Daniel's body as Prisca shrunk back, eyes flicking between Sarge and Daniel. By Mechan, this was either a dream or he was dead soon anyway. He picked up a can of fruit and threw it.

The can bounced off Sarge's shoulder. The man turned, his puzzled expression morphing into a thin twisted smile. Slaves rarely fought back, and Sarge enjoyed it when they did. He spun the lash in a tight circle and stepped towards Daniel. A second step sent a can flying across the hatch, leaving Sarge toppling onto the decking with a crash. A scream echoed between the metal walls as the impact shorted out the lash in his hand.

Sarge's belt pouch and gun holster filled Daniel's vision. As if in slow motion, he felt himself step forward. Saw his hand reach out for the pouch and rip out the collar key. He froze for a breath as Sarge groaned, trying to shake off the lash shock.

In a whirl of motion, Daniel grabbed Sarge's gun and stumbled to Prisca's side.

He unlocked her collar. "Get out." He nodded to the open bay door. Tree branches framed one side of the opening. "Jump. I'll be right behind you."

Prisca hesitated. Sarge groaned. Daniel pushed her

towards the door and turned.

Sarge was upright, his hand a blur of motion. Daniel jerked as pain coursed up his right arm to his shoulder. He dropped the gun and fell, rolling away from the frenzied soldier. In the doorway, he saw Prisca reaching for a branch.

Limbs spasmed as liquid lightning streaked along his thigh. He screamed. His left hand closed on a hunk of steel. The gun. He tried to raise his twitching hand. So heavy. Sarge's legs appeared, backed by the remaining ammunition case. Daniel lifted the gun a few inches. He fired.

Daniel forced an even pace down the school hallway. He couldn't be seen limping. He got past his parents last night by claiming illness. Not really a lie; it had been hours before the ringing in his ears from the explosion had subsided and his vision cleared. But if any teacher suspected a medical problem, they'd send him to a doctor. No way could he explain the blistering welts on his arm and thigh. And even mentioning the fighting machine would land him in the nut ward.

"Leave me alone." A girl's voice cut through the chatter of the students.

Up ahead, Cody had Priscilla backed up against a locker. "I think we oughta be friends." Cody's low voice sounded anything but friendly as it echoed down the hallway.

Daniel started to veer away. Stopped. Couldn't just walk away. And what's the worst that Cody could do? Pound him a little? Nothing compared to Sarge's whip.

Priscilla's eyes glanced at Daniel.

"Leave her alone!" Daniel broke into a gimping run. He grabbed Cody's shirt with his left hand and heaved the jerk away from Priscilla.

He heard a sharp intake of breath from Priscilla. Saw Cody's face go from surprise to a crooked smile.

It would hurt a little. But Cody would forget about Priscilla for a while.

Walt Socha is a recent retiree from the high tech silicon industry. He has short stories published in *Spaceports & Spidersilk, Beyond Centarui, Aurora Wolf, Aoife's Kiss' Cover of Darkness* anthology, and the 2015 Northwest Independent Writers Association's Anthology: *ASYLUM*. He continues to write sort stories while working on an Alternative History series set in the 11th Century. Walt lives in Portland, Oregon with his artist wife Gretha and two cats named Schiz and Zoid. More information on Walt's activities can be found at www.waltsocha.com.

STRANDS OF GRASS

By Renee Whittington

The field where the Battle of Kinjai took place three hundred years ago lies not far from my home. Nothing now remains visible of the battle's depredations. It is a wide expanse of tall grass that slopes down toward the land around it, like a cake fallen on one side. Orchards and farmland encircle it now.

Not a tree grows upon it, just acres of long, flowing grass that is green in the warm months and brown in the cold. The grass seems almost to whisper to itself as the wind blows over it. I can hear it as I lie in my bed each night.

When I was a young girl of ten years or so, Father would take me out to the battlefield sometimes, after my lessons were done for the day.

"See, Sekuri," he told me once, pointing toward the front of the plateau. "This is where General Changan made his last stand with his troops before they were cut down by the Yanji. Higher up is where we lost our mages, who were protected in the rear," he said. "That small rise to the north is where General Ruzan started his cavalry charge, but sadly, it was not enough. The Yanji sorcerers won that battle and the war, and it took us, all the Sahren people, over a century to defeat them and regain our freedom. What lesson can be learned from this?"

Father was very fond of asking me that question when he recounted history—I had known he would ask it from the moment he brought me to the battlefield and started to speak. I had noticed, even at my young age, that my older sister never anticipated the question. So I tried to think of an answer to the inevitable query before Father asked it.

The plateau was good, clear land for a battle; there was nowhere an army could hide for miles around. Had the Yanji tried to attack from the rear, the cliff would have been too high for arrows, and even levin-bolts might not have reached that high.

"There is no cover for anyone on the plateau, and our army was weak and outnumbered. They should have attacked the Yanji in secret, in small numbers, disrupted their supply lines, damaged their weapons, slain key officers. Instead, they tried to attack as a full army, and they couldn't maintain the attack. They were half-starved by then," I said, remembering the history I had been taught.

"Yes," Father said. "The generals, despite the army's wretched state, were still arrogant enough to think they could defeat an army four times their size, with tired troops, using outmoded tactics of honorable combat against those who were dishonorable. The deeper lesson is, 'Know your enemy, and know your people.' If you know your enemy well, you will know better how to defeat them." He shook his head. "We do not know how many unnamed people died in that battle or who they were; all we have are the names of the generals. But with only generals, there is no army. Remember that, when you grow old enough to lead troops, my daughter. Know and remember the people who fight for you, too. You might have to order their deaths, and they deserve better from you than for you to think of them as pieces on a shamati board, yes?"

"Yes, Father," I said slowly. Then I turned to him. "Does that make you sad, to know them well and have to send them out to fight?"

"It makes me very sad," he replied. "And it makes me a better general, I hope, because, if I must send my people to death, I want very much for it not to be a pointless death. And I want to make very certain that I seek all possible ways of preserving them before I conclude that sending them to death is the only way to succeed."

I nodded. Suddenly, it felt to me that being a general

was a terrible, frightening responsibility, and I wasn't sure I wanted it.

Today, I can hear the battlefield's grass whispering in the wind as I stand with my mother and sister at Father's funeral. Our hair is unbound, as is the hair of every soldier present. It whips against our faces, catches in armor, tangles about us in a flurry, as wild as grief can be.

It is eight years since the day Father spoke to me about knowing the troops well. I took his words to heart. The troops stand around us in a great crescent in their chain and leather armor, and I can name every one of them, and even some of their wives, husbands, and children. I am not old enough to be a general yet, but I can feel that the day will come. I do not wear armor today, but I feel the weight of their lives on me as heavily as if they were steel pauldrons on my shoulders. It is Father's bequest to me.

The priests in their saffron robes light sticks of pungent incense and chant funerary chants in a sonorous, beautiful harmony so deep I can feel it vibrating in my bones. Then the oldest priest bows low and hands Mother the torch. In a shaking but determined voice she offers a prayer and lights the funeral pyre, the final duty of a general's beloved. The flames roar up in a rush as the tinder burns, thrashing above the kindling in as great a frenzy as our hair and quilted silks. Above it all, I hear the rustling of the grass on the battlefield as the cold wind blasts at us.

My people are not given to the luxury of poetic expressions. But it feels to me in this moment that the battlefield grass quivers in the wind like the hair we unbind in grief—as if the earth, in its own way, mourns for those it holds in its embrace.

Renee Whittington is a children's blindness rehabilitation assistant living in Houston, Texas. She and her husband live in a home filled with entirely too many books—Hurray for eBooks! She has worked as a secretary in a parole office, as a medical transcriptionist, and as a summer intern at NASA's Johnson Spacecraft Center for several years, a long time ago. "Strands of Grass" is her first professional fiction sale. She has also been published in *Teatime in the Oleander Garden: A Collection of Poetry by Southern Women* and in *Mediphors* magazine.

IN OTHER WORDS

Lisa Timpf

Tall and thin, Mike Brownley grinned at his best friend Aubrey as he held the basketball. A quick fake to the left got Aubrey leaning, and Mike drove past for the layup.

"OK, you win this one," Aubrey said grudgingly. "Ready for a break?"

Out of breath, Mike could only nod as he dropped into one of the white plastic chairs set up courtside just for this purpose.

"What would you give to be at those talks?" Mike asked after a few moments.

Their fathers, part of the Special Forces unit of the Confederation of Nations, were currently assigned to support the negotiations with the Galavians. The black-furred humanoid aliens had cruised into Earth's solar system a month ago, and discussions had continued since.

"Wish I could have seen the pictures from their side," Aubrey said with a grin. Familiar with the process both as a result of his own research and information gleaned from his dad, he knew that the first step in building a language database was to show images from each side's planet and have individuals from each planet say out loud their word for that image. Aubrey was burning with curiosity about the images of their planet and culture that the Galavians would have provided.

"After the pictures, what comes next?" Mike asked. "I mean, I know you try to start with identifying each side's words for the same object, but then what?"

"They're using a special translation computer," Aubrey explained. "After the computer identifies common words for the same objects, members of each side read literature, news stories, and so on so the computer can also develop a sense of how words are organized into sentences, how ideas are expressed. When they figure they have enough information, the computer starts translating live conversation. They use an android linked to the computer for the face-to-face discussions; that makes it seem more personal."

"How well do you think it will work?" Mike's forehead furrowed.

"The computer has been shown to be reasonably accurate for Earth languages, but you're talking about human thought patterns," Aubrey said. "We hadn't developed this technology yet when the Ptomians came five years ago, and everyone saw what happened then."

Both boys were silent for a space, Aubrey thinking of his mother, a fighter pilot, who'd been a casualty in the last push by the aliens.

Concerned by the serious look on his friend's face, Mike rose to his feet.

"Rematch?" Mike waved the ball in Aubrey's direction.

Before Aubrey could respond, a commanding bark from Max, Aubrey's yellow Labrador Retriever, brought both boys to attention. The dog, who had been lying patiently beside the backyard basketball court, was suddenly interested in something at the front of the house, and even the boys could now hear the hum of a hover car coming in for a landing in the driveway.

"That'll be my dad," Mike commented as he reached for his zip-up hoodie.

The two friends headed for the gate leading from the back yard.

Sure enough, there was the Brownleys' silver hover car, sitting in front of Mike's house. Dark-haired Rupert Brownley stuck an arm out of the driver's side window to wave, while Aubrey's dad Cole popped out of the passenger side. Just returning from work, both men still wore their military uniforms.

"Talks go well today?" asked Aubrey.

"Slow, but with the translation computer we're making progress," Cole said, absently running his hand through his crew-cut silver hair. "We were finished calibrating the languages a couple of days ago, so it's coming along." Cole's face showed the strain of the day's efforts. "The next two weeks will be critical," he added. "We can't afford the mistakes that set off the conflict with the Ptomians. We just don't have the firepower left, nor can we afford the damage, frankly."

Mike's usually cheerful face was somber. He only needed to look at the skyline, recognize the gaps where the landmarks he'd known all his life were missing or damaged, to know the truth of those words.

"See you tomorrow," he said to Aubrey with a nod as he hopped into the recently-vacated passenger side of the sleek hover car.

The next day was a Saturday, but both Cole and Rupert had to work. There was no time to waste with the negotiations, and the heat from the media and the public was mounting. The sooner the two sides could come to agreement, the better.

When Rupert arrived to collect Cole, Mike clambered out of the hover car, lugging his paintball gear in a gym bag.

"Have fun, boys," Cole called out as he boarded the

vehicle. Clad in her uniform, Aubrey's older sister, Jackie, had already climbed into the rear passenger side seat and was fiddling with her shoulder-length brown hair as she waited for liftoff. Working as a first-level runner at the talks, she too had to work this Saturday.

"We'll be missing our third for paintball today," Mike said with a shrug, gesturing toward Jackie, who was a crack shot. "May as well head over anyway and see who we can scare up."

Aubrey watched the hover car lift, turn, and swing out of sight. The whole, long summer stretched ahead of them, and with all the tensions from the talks, it was clear there wouldn't be a lot of family time in the near future. Cadets' meetings had been suspended, too, with the leaders caught up in the negotiations. There'd be a lot of time to fill, Aubrey thought as he shouldered his gear bag.

He looked longingly at his family's Goosewing II gold hover car as he walked beside Mike down the driveway. He'd just gotten his license a few weeks ago, but with the fuel rationing still in place, taking transit made a lot more sense. Besides, their fathers were trying to set an example by carpooling to conserve fuel, so he and Mike ought to follow suit. Parking was always a hassle in the downtown section anyway.

Aubrey and Mike walked the short distance to the tube stop, paid their fare, and boarded. Not unusual for a Saturday morning, the tube was fairly full and they reluctantly squeezed in beside a young man who looked around their own age and close to Aubrey's height, a good six inches shorter than Mike. The stranger was wearing a toque pulled low over his face, sunglasses—unusual for the somewhat overcast day—and a surgical mask, customary for someone in the crowded city who had a slight cough, as a courtesy to avoid infecting others.

Aubrey studied the stranger out of the corner of his eye, not wanting to stare. Odd. Now that he looked more closely, Aubrey noted that the stranger didn't just have his face shielded, he was completely covered head to toe—a scarf closed the gap between the surgical mask and his hoodie, and ill-fitting jeans covered his legs down to high-top runners. He also wore black leather gloves.

The stranger shifted position, and Aubrey let out a gasp. When the boy beside him moved, a gap opened up between the gloves and the hoodie, showing an arm covered with dense black fuzz. Aubrey elbowed Mike and jerked his head toward the stranger. Noting the same thing, Mike's left eyebrow shot up.

The stranger was one of the Galavians!

When Mike and Aubrey stood to get off the bus, the stranger rose too. Aubrey's heart beat faster. If they played this right, they might actually get to meet a Galavian, face to face!

Once they stepped onto the sidewalk, the stranger seemed uncertain which direction to go. Aubrey waited till the area around the tube stop had cleared, then stuck out his hand.

"I'm Aubrey," he said as the stranger slowly extended his own hand for a tentative greeting. "And we know who you are."

Half an hour later, Aubrey and Mike had company as they walked through the entrance of the paintball gym. The Galavian they'd met on the tube turned out to be Vrynx Vcznk, the son of the lead negotiator, Zmyd. Vrynx had decided to take an excursion from the compound where the Galavians were staying, hoping to learn more about Earth culture. He was cautious enough to wear a disguise, recognizing that not all Earth residents were receptive to dealing with the aliens.

After a brief explanation sketched out mainly through gestures and a few words, Vrynx indicated his desire to join Mike and Aubrey in their paintball game, noting that all Galavians were encouraged to become expert marksmen and markswomen from an early age. This encouragement, Aubrey and Mike gathered, had ramped up after the Galavians had suffered severe damage to their planet and population at the hands of a Ptomian invasion force.

Aubrey quickly handled the rental of the required

gear for Vrynx, his mind racing as he and Mike assisted the Galavian in discretely suiting up.

Just as Aubrey and Mike made the final adjustments to Vrynx's gear, muscular Marcus Howerby, captain of the opposing team, strutted over.

"New player this week, I see," he said, sizing up Vrynx with a penetrating stare. "No matter. You'll still lose." He waved a hand dismissively as he turned to go.

"As I recall," Mike said with a sarcastic grin, "we won last week."

"Whatever," Marcus grunted. "We're ready whenever you are."

Two hours later, the boys walked out of the paintball facility, with Vrynx's street disguise firmly in place.

Aubrey's head was spinning. Not only had they won, they had thrashed Marcus and his two friends soundly, thanks to Vrynx, who had proven to be agile, quick-thinking, and deadly accurate. If all the Galavians could shoot like him, getting a treaty in place was all the more important.

"Weather is nice," Aubrey gestured to the sky. "We can walk back to the compound." He pointed to his feet. Vrynx had picked up many words in the English language, but he was far from fluent, so gestures and short phrases supported the communication process.

"Yes," Vrynx said simply. "I like that."

As they walked, signs of the Ptomian conflict were everywhere—stately trees shattered, houses with roofs blown off, abandoned storefronts.

Vrynx gestured to one of the shattered, boarded-up houses. "Our planet, damage like this also."

Aubrey and Mike nodded.

Near one of the parks that had somehow emerged from the war unharmed, a gray squirrel ran up a tree. Vrynx stopped and stared.

"Small," he muttered.

"Small?" Mike questioned. "Squirrel. Normal size for us."

"Our planet, much larger." With his hands, Vrynx sketched out an animal the size of a horse. "Fly from tree to tree. Sometimes, we ride."

Just then, Aubrey's phone buzzed. He pulled out the device, read the screen, and turned pale.

"What is it?" Mike asked.

"Message from Jackie," Aubrey said tersely. "There's trouble with the talks."

Vrynx looked directly at his two new friends. "I worry," he said. "Something wrong with words."

"Words?" Aubrey asked.

"Words not correct, sometimes," Vrynx said carefully. "I listen radio, TV, I learn some English. Machine make wrong words. Maybe problem."

Mike and Aubrey exchanged glances.

"Change of plan," Mike said. "We need to get to the negotiation chamber."

"I come, too," Vrynx sounded determined, and neither Mike nor Aubrey argued.

The three boys hurried as quickly as they could to the compound where the talks were being held. Outside the main gate, their progress was slowed as they worked their way past a crowd of protesters, who were holding signs with messages like, "No Talks Are Good Talks," and "Remember the Ptomians".

"It's the Earth First Alliance," Aubrey explained to Vrynx. "I'm sorry. Some folks here on Earth don't think we should negotiate with your people."

"Our planet, same issue," Vrynx said calmly.

"Don't they get it?" Mike snarled. "It was because we couldn't come to terms with the Ptomians that we ended up in a war."

Aubrey's shoulders tensed as a loud, angry buzz arose from the crowd. He crouched in a ready position, determined to defend his new friend if it came to that, then noticed that no-one was looking in their direction. Instead, they were looking up at the sky.

The stark, crisp lines of the Galavian space vessel, which had been orbiting so high up it was barely visible, were now distinct in the sky. Also distinct were a significant number of the Conferation's Cobra fighter jets, looking small as gnats beside the alien ship.

"We need to hurry," Aubrey muttered.

Pushing through the crowd, they worked their way to the building's ornate entrance, where the double doors bore the crest of the Confederation of Nations. For the sons of Cole Johnson and Rupert Brownley, both cadets in their own right, entry to the general area where the talks were being held was difficult but not impossible. Once inside the building, Vrynx took off his surgical mask and glasses to reveal his identity, and he was also allowed in.

"This way." Aubrey took the lead as the trio sped toward the viewing area.

When they arrived, it didn't take long to size up the situation. As each negotiating team made their comments in turn, the four-foot-high translation android in the middle of the table uttered a string of sounds in the other group's language.

As the talks continued, the body language of each side made it clear that anger and frustration were rising.

It took only ten minutes of this before it seemed some kind of physical conflict was brewing. Vrynx stood up suddenly.

"Different words," he said with absolute certainty. "Computer say different words."

"We need to tell someone," Aubrey said.

Before Aubrey finished talking, Vrynx was sprinting to the lower door, and from there, racing out into the chamber. Aubrey and Mike, stumbling in their haste, were right behind him.

Whenever he thought back on the events that followed, Aubrey marveled that he'd had the nerve to proceed despite the icy blue-eyed glare his father initially fixed on him. He also realized how incredibly lucky they were that the guards stationed around the room were disciplined enough to refrain from shooting when the three boys burst into the room unannounced.

While Vrynx talked urgently to his father, Aubrey and Mike told Cole, Rupert, and the other members of the Earth negotiation team about Vrynx's suspicions.

Fortunately, unshakeably calm Mbana, nicknamed Mab, had been selected as the chairperson for the proceedings. The tall, solidly-built Afro-Caribbean had seen a lot in his sixty years—including a five-year stint on the lunar colony—and was prepared to give the boys the benefit of the doubt. Ever observant, he too had noted the increasing tension in the room, and this, at least, would provide an explanation for why things were going so wrong, despite good intentions.

"I suggest we look into this matter," he said. "Let's declare a recess and get started again tomorrow."

To avoid any risk of further misunderstanding, Vrynx translated this message for the Galavians. At the same time, the translation android interpreted what Mab had just said.

The Galavians turned as one to stare at the android.

"My idea right," Vrynx said after a brief pause. "Computer said, 'We have no common ground'—not what you said at all."

Amid the hubbub that burst out in the chamber in two languages after that comment, Rupert and Cole exchanged glances.

"We need to get to the bottom of this," Rupert snapped. "I'll get my team started."

Too anxious to go home, Aubrey and Mike hung out in the chambers while Rupert and Cole sped off into the labyrinth-like building. After some heated discussion with his father, Vrynx drifted over to join them.

"He ask our ship to move back into space," Vrynx told Aubrey.

"If we can't trust the computer, what now?" Mike asked worriedly.

"We need to work the old fashioned way," Aubrey commented thoughtfully. "We've been relying on a machine to translate for us, but we may be better off making sure we truly understand each other."

"Easy for you to say, you're good at languages." Mike snorted.

"Aubrey right," said Vrynx. "Start at beginning. Truly understand. Better."

"How did you pick up English, anyway?" Mike asked.

"Listen radio waves. My hobby," Vrynx smiled.

"Oh, like a ham radio operator?" Mike said.

"You call me pig?"

"No, ham radio operator means someone who works with radios as a hobby," Mike replied.

Vrynx's shoulders rose and fell in a sigh. "Many confusions," he said, raising his hand to his head.

It took Rupert's security team three hours to track down the details, but it soon became clear that the garbled translation was no accident.

"Looks like the work of the Earth First Alliance," Rupert explained to Cole and the other Earth leaders. "They hacked into the program and set it up to make the translation increasingly insulting and divisive."

"Their motivation is clear, then," Mab commented.

"More to it than that," Rupert said. "We've suspected for some time that the Alliance is actually linked to the Ptomians. They most of all would want to ensure the various other civilizations don't join forces."

"Why would anyone from Earth support the Ptomians,

after what they did to us?" Mike's voice shook with anger.

"Everyone has their motivations," Cole explained. "Their families may have been threatened. They may have been promised things. We don't really know at this point."

"What we do know is that the talks have to start from the beginning—without machines this time, so we can be certain," Rupert said. "It'll need more manpower and be slower, but it's the only way."

"Well, boys, looks like the cadet force will get put to work," Cole told Mike and Aubrey. "We'll need to cooperate with our guests at all levels, and that includes getting to know as much as we can about their culture."

Mike and Aubrey exchanged grins with Vrynx.

"You know what this means," Mike said, once the two were on their own.

"Not much spare time," Aubrey groaned, pretending to be upset.

"No, it means we have a new hobby, when we can find a few minutes," Mike said, pausing for effect. "Riding lessons."

"Whatever for?" Aubrey rolled his eyes.

"For when we get to see those giant flying squirrels in person."

Lisa Timpf is a freelance writer who lives in Simcoe, Ontario. Her creative non-fiction, fiction, and poetry have been published in a variety of venues, including *Chicken Soup for the Soul: Christmas in Canada, New Myths, Outposts of Beyond, The Martian Wave, Scifaikuest, and Third Wednesday.* Lisa enjoys organic gardening, hiking in the woods, and contemplating the stars.

ANOTHER SUNSET

by Anne E. Johnson

[KI]

A shaft of hot pink sunlight blasted along the edge of the doorway.

"It will blind me yet," Mama complained.

Chara laughed. "Just turn your head, Mama." She grabbed the water jug. "I'm going to the well."

"You're a good girl," she heard Mama say as she closed the door behind her.

Squinting against the light didn't bother Chara. Every day she looked forward to watching the sun melt down into Mount Aconcagua. It was her favorite moment in daily life. "It's even worth carrying you," she told the water jug.

"There goes silly Chana, dreaming again," said one of the village women.

"Look," another woman clucked, "she's walked right

past the well."

"Maybe she's planning to fill her jug with fine evening air."

Chana didn't mind their teasing. "Blessings to your families," she called, circling around the well. Then off she raced to her favorite rock, clambered up, and took a seat. She placed the empty water jug carefully beside her.

The setting was almost perfect. Only one thing could improve it: Teo.

[SHŌ]

Click, click. Chana smiled at the familiar sound.

"Beautiful colors tonight." Teo held up the camera hanging from a strap around his neck. "Beautiful girls, too," he added, snapping Chana's picture.

"Oh, you stop." She batted her eyelashes and heaved a dramatic sigh. "Don't get distracted, lover boy, or we'll miss the sunset."

Teo kissed her and nodded. "You are right, as ever."

They sat quietly, watching the west bleed crimson and magenta. The only sounds were the clicks from Teo's camera and the muffled signs of village life behind them.

Chana let her head's weight press into Teo's bicep. "Look how the horizon curves," she said.

"The great circle of land and sea," Teo replied, lowering his camera. "Imagine how many people have sat and watched the sun set today."

"But at different times all over the world," Chana said. After watching Teo focus and click a few more pictures, she put her hand on his arm. "What was it like before people knew the Earth was round?"

Teo grinned. "I supposed they worried about falling off the edges."

"Yes, I think they did." Chana did not join in Teo's laughter; the idea fascinated her. "How long do you think it took for everyone to believe in a horizon curving to infinity?" When Teo kept on shooting, she continued. "Or did it happen all in one day? Someone showed the world absolute proof that you can't fall off the edge of the world? No, in the past so many people's minds could not have been changed at once. You need computers for that, right? Teo?"

[TEN]

Teo faced away from her, his shoulders squeezed upward. He didn't move. He seemed to be holding his breath.

"What's wrong?" Chana asked in a fearful whisper.

"They're incredible."

Before Chana could ask what he meant, she saw the three birds. At least, she thought they were birds for a few seconds. Then she saw through their wings into the tangerine glow of the sun's last gasp. Lines of intense green lights outlined the birds' bodies.

"Airplanes?" Teo guessed.

"Too small even for a child to fly in." While Chana spoke, the bird-planes sank steadily. Columns of steam blasted from their underbellies; they landed, smoothly as falling seed pods, on the scrubby grass.

"Let's go closer and see," Chana urged.

The fear in Teo's eyes held her back.

"Right," she soothed him. "We'll watch from here."

The bird-planes rocked back on their ends. Their middles split and unfurled like hides before tanning. Only these hides were nearly clear, and they glowed a spooky, pale green.

"Chana!" Teo hissed. "Look."

As if she could do anything but look! Still, she gaped harder as a little being crawled out of each wrapping. "Like living quartz rock," said Chana. She tried to understand their shapes, but they changed and changed.

"Jelly in a bag," said Teo.

The creatures bent down, arched up, spun in a complete circle. The dim twilight picked out white veins through their lavender bodies. One of them angled its bulbous top toward Chana.

"They're aliens. Real aliens." Her voice came out as barely more than breath.

Teo nodded slightly. "I know."

[KETSU]

A little lavender visitor rolled and dragged its way forward. Even though it had no eyes, Chana was sure it stared at her.

A spray of orange-yellow at the horizon signaled the end of the day's sun. The ground's grays battled with blackish green, fighting disappearance. The aliens must have known: they squirmed back toward their little ships. Chana realized that their visit, like the sun's, would soon be history.

"Teo." She spoke firmly so he would listen. "Your camera. Take pictures now."

With shaking hands, Teo raised the camera. Click. The visitors froze. Click. They hurried to their ships. Click, click. Climbed in. Click. Green lights on. Click, click, click. Taking off, rising, silhouetted. Click. Vanished.

The sun vanished, too. Teo took Chana's hand.

"In the future," she said, "a boy and girl will stand here."

Teo kissed her shoulder. "Yes. And they'll ask, 'What was it like when people didn't believe aliens visited Earth?'"

"And they'll wonder," Chana whispered close to his ear, "who took those pictures that made everyone believe, all at once, that alien visits are as obvious and true as sunrise and sunset."

Wrapping her arms around Teo, she stared up at the pale stars. "I should bring home the water jug," she sighed.

"I'll see you here tomorrow." She spoke those words to the sun. And to anyone else it cared to invite.

Anne E. Johnson lives in Brooklyn, NY. She writes speculative and historical fiction for kids, teens, and adults. Dozens of her short stories have been published, and many can be read in her collection *Things from Other Worlds*. Her novel-length fiction includes *Ebenezer's Locker, Green Light Delivery,* and *Blue Diamond Delivery.* Learn more at AnneEJohnson.com.

MECHANIKA

By Mara Dabrishus

The buses moved in a column, winding away from smoke stacks that belched warm plumes into the driving snow. Zoya sat by the window on the third bus, eyes closed, shivering on her frost-covered plastic seat, gloved fingers tucked between her thermal-clad legs. Snow shifted across the road, wind blowing it back and forth, whistling around the bus as it jostled its contents and received weary sighs in return. Ice crystals hung in the air, sparking in the twilight of a polar night that bathed the crumbling old city in blue.

Zoya shifted away from her seatmate, a bulky man who smelled like grease and melted metal, although there was little chance she smelled much better. The bus reeked of workers, soot-streaked and exhausted. If Zoya opened her eyes, she would be met with walls of snow stacked high along the road, hiding the feet of abandoned buildings.

Snow capped the windows, sloped over roofs, burst out of doors left open.

Only snow lived here.

Ahead of them was the gate, a puncture hole in the wall that wrapped the new city in a tight embrace. Above it was the old era sign in blocky blue text: Норильск. Norilsk. Beneath it: ЗАТО. Closed.

The buses came to a whining halt, the engines rumbling. The doors hissed open, letting in a blast of frigid air that Zoya felt through all her layers. The NKVD boarded, as they always did, in pairs. One officer for each side of the bus.

The door stayed open during inspection, snow collecting on the stairs as each passenger was barked at to lift their right wrist. Lift, scan, beep. Lift, scan, beep. Zoya listened until the heavy footfalls made their way to her seatmate. Lift, scan, beep.

She waited, eyes closed, for the demand.

"Lift your right wrist," the officer commanded, voice bouncing on the frozen walls. Zoya flinched at the tone, and mourned having to remove her hands from warmth. She hesitated—a mistake. The split second of stillness was enough, and the officer found her elbow, forcibly yanking her hands from their position tucked between her thighs.

The bus fell into silence as her glove was peeled off, dropped onto the muddy floor.

Scan.

"Zoya Ivanova," the officer said, gripping her wrist harder, expecting a reaction.

Zoya opened her eyes.

Beep.

Pink stained snow covered cars left in the courtyards along Pavlova Ulica, created discolored mounds along the stretch of apartments—an old era rectangular block painted lemon yellow. Workers scurried home, huddled in their coats against the rising wind that threatened to knock their feet out from under them. Zoya stumbled into the narrow plaza entrance of building 21, stopping along the way to dig for the vodka she kept stashed in the snowdrift nearest to the door.

The liquid burned cold in her mouth, followed with a flash of welcome heat. Zoya pressed her lips together, replacing the cap and pushing the bottle back into its hidey-hole on her way to the open building door.

Muddy tracks trailed down the hallway, the carpet worn down to concrete. The once bright green walls now dimmed by dust and time. Her neighbor sat slumped against his front door. A half-empty vodka bottle was cradled in his hands as his head tipped forward toward his chest. Zoya stepped over his long legs and bent to wake him, hand on his shoulder.

"It's too cold in the hallway, Nikolai," she said after he

yanked his head back, knocking it against the door. "Go inside."

She found his key on her chain and unlocked his door, watching him roll onto his knees and crawl inside without so much as a word. It was their unspoken understanding. Nikolai would arrive home too drunk to comprehend his keys, and Zoya would let him in when she found him, as she almost always did.

When she turned to her own door, wondering what state she would find her mother in this evening, her phone trilled in a way that made her heart stop. It was a noise she hadn't heard in a week as she waited for news. She groped for it, the face of the phone lighting up with the message.

You just made things harder.

Zoya huffed, irritation flooding her.

Explain, she typed.

No reply was immediately forthcoming, and forever impatient, Zoya shoved the phone back in her pocket. She opened the door to her mother lying on the kitchen floor, giggling at the ceiling, her graying black hair swirling amidst the crumbs that littered the linoleum. The UV lamp blazed in the corner of the living room, lighting up the contents of her stash on the coffee table. Zoya passed her mother without comment, turning off the UV lamp before returning to the kitchen.

"Mama," Zoya said, sitting on her knees next to her mother's head, picking a piece of cereal out of her hair. "You know what the NKVD will do if they find you this way."

Mama's giggling reached a fever pitch. "Put me down like a dog?" she asked through a smile. "They are the dogs."

Zoya did not argue that, not when her mother's only crime was being the wife of an innocent man, convicted on gossip. The drugs, on the other hand, were punishable by death. They sowed weakness among the workers, and weak workers could not survive the mines. Mama insisted she was clean on her workdays, but Zoya suspected otherwise when all of her few hours off were spent on the kitchen floor.

"Get up," Zoya commanded, taking Mama's hand and standing. Mama's head tipped back as she laughed. "Get up!"

Mama yanked her hand away, falling back and spitting. "Do not tell your mother what to do."

"I must if she spends all day on the floor."

Mama lashed out a foot, kicking and hitching into a scream. Zoya jumped back, raising her hands in surrender.

Her phone trilled, and Zoya was happy to retreat, pulling it from her pocket.

Meet. Mechanika.

How will I find you? she typed.

We will find you.

Under the frozen layer of tundra twisted the mines. The oldest, long since abandoned, curved under the city, and when an intrepid child found an emergency shaft into the pitch-black cauldron it was transformed into Mechanika. Electrical lines were wired, a trickle of running water supplied, all under the knowing eye of the NKVD.

Let them have their fun, someone must have said. So it was.

Zoya dressed in something appropriate. Black boots, thick tights that sagged around her hips, and a black sweater made of dense wool so long it passed as a dress. She shrugged into her coat and pulled her dark hair out of the collar, letting it hang down her back as she glanced at herself in the mirror.

She looked like death. Pale skin and dark smudges around her hollow eyes. The polar night was taking its toll.

Without saying goodbye to Mama, Zoya let herself out of the apartment and softly locked the door. Mechanika was a long walk into the night, and she wrapped her neck and face with a scarf that was damp seconds after stepping foot in the snow.

In the pale blue light, she could make out the smoke-stacks through the storm. The trio loomed over the candy-colored buildings around her, stark reminders that captivity was her life—if the wall and the razor wire weren't reminder enough.

Zoya was going to leave this place. If she couldn't get out by following the rules, she had to find another way. For as long as Zoya could remember, the wall cut them off from the rest of the country. No roads or rail connected to the mainland, and no flights had left with citizens since the last test took the best and brightest of Zoya's classmates to freedom. The rest of them were meant to work, to mine the world's largest nickel deposits out of the destroyed tundra.

According to the test, Zoya wasn't the best or brightest of Norilsk. So she would work at The Combine, taking care of the machines until she grew sick or old. When Mama wasn't seeing stars on the ceiling, she told Zoya that it was better than most people got. She knew the machines. Her father had taught her that much before he'd died. At least she wasn't in the mines.

But she was still here, imprisoned in Norilsk's winter.

The building sitting atop the elevator to Mechanika was a peeling rusty red, its steps to the front door crumbling. Zoya stepped inside gingerly, watching her feet, so preoccupied she ran into the back of the line.

"Watch out, now," the girl in front of her laughed, grabbing Zoya's wrist to steady them both. Her clothes were all sparkles, boots ending in spiked heels that pushed her well above Zoya's height. Glitter swept across her eyelids, and the tips of her white blond hair were chalked red. Zoya mumbled an apology, but the girl waved it off.

"I'm Irina," she said, whispering conspiratorially as if her name was a dark secret.

Zoya whispered her name right back as the elevator arrived, the metal gate cranking back to allow the next flood of people. Irina pulled Zoya into the overcrowded space, pushing the gate closed behind them. With a mechanical shriek, the elevator began its descent, sinking into the earth.

Hooking her fingers around the grate, Zoya breathed in the lingering scent of metal through the heavy perfume of the crowd. Irina, who chattered about meeting her friends for someone's birthday, smelled the way Zoya had imagined summer would smell, undercut by the wafting air of the ancient mine.

"I will buy you a shot," Irina declared, Mechanika's thump and pull beginning to reverberate over the grinding of the elevator. Zoya, heart thumping quickly, ignored Irina as she watched the party come into full view.

The mine was strung with lights, tiny white lines dangling along the curling ceiling while strobes flashed drunkenly over dancers. Cages hung from the ceiling, and dancers within crawled and climbed the bars. Puffs of smoke lifted from the crowd, acrid like the rain. Zoya backed away from the grate when the elevator jerked to a halt, letting someone else open it. People streamed around her, dispersing into the party like ravenous wolves.

Zoya stepped off and stood stalk still.

"Have you never been to Mechanika?" Irina asked, giving her a quizzical stare.

"Yes," Zoya said, scanning the crowd. "Of course."

"Then what's the problem?" Irina put a hand on her hip. "I said I'd buy you a shot, and I'm following through."

"I'm looking for someone," Zoya said, clipped. "I have no time for this."

Irina tilted her head, the glitter on her eyes sparking under the strobes. Then she pressed close, whispering into Zoya's ear, "I can take you to Volk, Zoya Ivanova."

Zoya pushed her away, catching Irina's slow smile, as if she took pleasure in surprising Volk's guests.

"Prove it," Zoya demanded.

"You were one percentage point off from joining the rest of those darlings on the latest flight, yes?" Irina asked, looking bored. She ran her fingers through the red tips of her hair. "You couldn't buy your way onto that flight, but you know something worthwhile because Volk wouldn't bother otherwise." She stopped fiddling with her hair. "Am I right?"

Zoya sighed, unimpressed but uneager to drag up her motives, which were so much larger than one percentage point. Irina raised an eyebrow, waiting.

"Take me to Volk, then," she said and followed as Irina wordlessly turned and wound through the crowd.

Mechanika rumbled and flashed, dancers barely moving out of the way for Irina to cut a path. The music stuttered and switched to something intensely popular, wild shouts rising up in the crowd. Zoya ducked under flailing arms and sidestepped around a couple intimately wound up in each other in the middle of the dance floor.

Irina skimmed around the edge of the makeshift bar, glancing behind her only once to make sure Zoya kept up. She pushed open a heavy steel door behind the bar, the metal screeching in protest.

"Down there," she said, motioning to the metal grate stairs that descended into near total darkness.

Zoya took one look at it and wanted desperately to laugh. She grasped the impulse and crushed it, refusing to let the dark scare her. She lived in Norilsk. Norilsk was the dark.

Reaching into her pocket, she pulled out her phone and turned it on, shining it into the hole.

"Are you coming?" Zoya asked.

Irina smiled. "No, darling," she said, kissing her on the temple. "I did my part. The rest is for you alone. You'll find Volk at the end of the hallway. Be impressive. Volk does not do this for everyone."

Zoya already knew that much. The messages she'd

received hardly played the concerned citizen. The Wolf of Norilsk spoke with her because she had something he wanted, and in return he would grant her escape.

She gripped the phone a little harder and headed down, pointing the beam of light at the crusty floor. Grit popped and scraped under her boots. When she turned the corner, faint light cast down the hall, illuminating the walls decorated with illegal resistance posters, brittle old photos of young people posing with Kalashnikovs during the Combine Strike when Zoya was a child, and a torn flag. Zoya passed the beam over it all, looking at the photos in awe. It was what she assumed a museum to be like, old things put on display like this.

A shadow fell across the hall, causing Zoya to shift the light abruptly to a boy maybe only a few years older than herself. He squinted, raising his hand to block his eyes. She turned off the light.

"Seriously?" she asked, shoving the phone into her coat pocket. "You're Volk?"

"What were you expecting?" he asked her, crossing his arms. She could not make him out as easily with the light behind him, so she pushed past into his lit chamber.

It was an old office, windowless and dry. It smelled like dust and metal. Earthy things. Lights were strung across the ceiling, like the rest of Mechanika. The walls were covered in maps, notes and photos pinned to corkboards.

Candles flickered on the table, next to warm cheese in its wrapper and an open bottle of vodka. A UV lamp sat unused in the corner by a torn leather sofa that looked original to the room.

"This is not a good space to hide," she said bluntly, turning around to face him and stopping short. He watched her from the doorway, looking at her curiously. "What?"

He shook his head. "Nothing. You are Zoya Ivanova and I am Volk. How I get out of here in moments of crisis is not your concern."

"It could be if you're helping me."

"If I am helping you is still quite up to debate," he said, striding into the room then and closing the door behind him. "Your stunt on the bus this evening put you on the watch list."

"And?"

"It makes it harder to hide you," Volk said, leaning against the desk. "It makes it harder to decide if you're worth it in the end."

Zoya pursed her lips, then took off her damp scarf, unwinding it and throwing it on the sofa, followed by her coat. Volk watched her impassively.

"Please, make yourself at home," he said, nodding to the sofa. She let his sarcasm go, approaching him and stopping short of the desk.

"What makes me worth it, exactly?" she asked. "I am not a fool. This isn't free."

"No," he agreed, pushing a hand into unkempt black hair. "It's not."

She looked down at the tabletop, noticing another old photo lying on top of a stack of papers as though forgotten. Her eyes caught on the men in the photo, standing around a lorry stacked high with food. Her father was among them, the spitting image of how she remembered him.

"What is the meaning of this?" she asked softly, picking up the photo, noticing the man that stood next to her father had to be related to Volk. The similarities were too many, in the sharp jaw and straight nose, thick black hair and same curving mouth.

"It is what it looks like," Volk said, and Zoya threw the photo down, anger cutting through her awe.

"Then tell me what it looks like," she snapped at him. "My father was a mechanic in The Combine. He wasn't . . . ."

"Nationalist," Volk replied. "He was a Nationalist. He led them, and he died with them."

Zoya laughed, backing away from him. "And here I've gone my whole life without knowing. Of course, that makes so much sense."

"How do you think you're here at all if not for Viktor Ivanov?"

She gave him a scathing look. "My father . . ."

"Your mother forbade anyone speak of it to you," Volk interrupted. "You were too young when he died to know the truth, only that he died at The Combine, which is true for all intents and purposes."

Zoya sat down with a rush on the sofa, the leather squeaking under her weight, and put her head in her hands. Volk walked across the room, squatting down in front of her. For several moments he was silent, watching the space between their feet.

"We played as kids," he said, gruffly, as though he didn't want to admit it. "You were three. I barely remember it myself."

Zoya snorted, laughing into her fingers and wiped the backs of her hands against her eyes. "Says the people smuggler."

He smiled grimly, looking at her with his forearms resting on his knees. She leaned back and shook her head.

"Let's say it's true," she said. "It still wouldn't be enough for you, would it? There's a price to helping me. What do you want?"

Volk stood up. "Codes," he said. "Door codes to all three plants. All that you can find."

Zoya nodded slowly. "Easy enough. What will you do in return?"

"Cut out your microchip," he said leaning down and

pressing his thumb against the inside of her right wrist. She flinched and drew away, his hand falling. "I have a friend on the train to Dudinka. You'll be smuggled out of the city by rail and put on the icebreaker Skopa with the rest of the freight. It's scheduled to arrive in Hamburg in two weeks' time. From there you have two options: forget all about this or do as your father did."

"And what's that?" she asked, standing up, steeling herself.

"Don't forget," he said and winked.

The storm continued into the next day. Snow came down yellow, streaked with gray soot. Zoya walked home in it, sliding every few steps with a gust of wind powerful enough to drag her into traffic. She steadied herself and kept trudging forward, shoulders up against the chill and heart pounding anxiously in her throat.

As she predicted, gathering the codes for Volk was simple. So much of the machines were operated by computer, like so many of the doors. Fixing a crusher machine, while more complicated than fixing a lock, still involved the same tools. It was only a few different clicks, and the codes were laid bare.

Zoya hid the flash drive in her boot, tucked into her sock so it nestled up against her skin. Boots tended to be ignored during random frisks. There were so many other parts of the body to grab.

Her phone chimed, and she dragged it out into the blistering wind.

?

She typed out, *Yes.*

A second passed.

Bring what you need. No more.

Turning the corner of her apartment building, she stopped to brush away the extra layer of snow from the vodka bottle and took a larger than normal gulp. The vodka raced to do its work, making what she would have to do now more bearable.

Zoya went through her routine, letting Nikolai into his apartment like a lost dog and turning to face her own door like she was walking to the gallows. The flash drive was warm against her ankle, a whisper of encouragement.

She opened the door to an empty kitchen, but the retching noise from the bathroom was all Zoya needed to know. Closing the door behind her, she made her way across the small living space and found Mama curled over the toilet, two bottles of vodka sitting on the floor. Mama's tangled hair knotted across her shoulders as she heaved.

Zoya stood still, watching. When Mama was done, she leaned against the far wall and breathed a sigh, reaching for the less empty bottle and drinking the taste out of her mouth.

"Tell me about Papa," Zoya said.

"No," Mama replied.

"I know who he was," Zoya said, pushing her hands deeper into her pockets. "Nothing you've done has protected me from not knowing."

Mama pushed a shaking hand into her hair and pulled at it, a whine traveling up her throat. "No," she said, repetitively, pulling at her hair. "No. He is dead, and you will not slander his name."

"Tell me," Zoya pushed.

"No!" Mama shouted, throwing the bottle against the porcelain tub, glass and liquor exploding across the floor. Mama pressed her fingers against her face, curling into a tight ball, high pitched cries muffled into her hands.

Zoya started forward and stopped, thought better of it. She left Mama crying over the broken glass, retreating to the bedroom they shared. She'd stashed her bag in the closet, far enough back that Zoya stood on tiptoe from the sagging mattress to hook a finger around the strap. It hit the floor with a thud, catching a water-stained envelope on its way down. Photos scattered out of it, flipping to the floor.

Faces stared up at her from the photographs, smiles that she didn't remember happening in her family. With a pause, Zoya crouched down and gathered the pictures one by one, filing through her laughing mother, her beaming father, Zoya when she was a mere child. They were not so broken then.

She paused on a battered photo of her father. He was holding her, maybe just a toddler, bundled in down and wool against the arctic wind. Next to them was the man from the photo in Volk's room under the Mechanika, gangly boy with dark hair sitting on his shoulders.

Zoya flipped the photo over, hoping for some identifying name and found light pencil marks on the slippery backing.

Viktor and Zoya. Dmitry and Alexei.

Zoya traced her fingers over the words. They were written in her mother's precise handwriting from before.

Alexei.

She turned the photo over again and studied it, traced the lines in the face of a small boy who would grow up to be Volk. The Wolf of Norilsk. She looked at herself as a child, face barely showing through the coat, and could remember nothing.

Mama's soft sobs drifted down the hallway, reminding Zoya that her questions had gone unanswered. Hastily, she threw the rest of the photos together and shoved them into her bag, keeping the photograph of Volk in her cupped palm. She paused by the bathroom on her way to the door, but she couldn't make herself look in on Mama. If she did, she knew what she would see. What she would see might tempt her to stay, and there could be no staying.

She hiked her bag onto her shoulder and whispered down the hallway, "I'm going now, Mama."

Zoya did not wait for an answer, and when she reached the door, the sobs had stopped. She hoped that somehow her absence would bring her mother peace, a little less of a reminder of what she'd lost. She swallowed down the instinctual urge to turn around, to check on her, and left the apartment.

When she headed into the storm, she recovered the vodka from its hole, tucking it under her arm. The walk to Mechanika was brisk, snow falling in large flakes and breaking apart on her chapped cheeks. The elevator carried her down into the bowels of the party, and she moved through the crush of people without ever seeing them, dropping down into Volk's narrow hallway without the light and without Irina guiding the way.

She appeared in his doorway snow wet and shivering, throwing the bag down at her feet. He looked up at her and said, "Codes?"

"Hello to you, too," she said to him, bending down and fishing the drive out of her sock. She tossed it to him, and he caught it.

"You're efficient," he said, turning to push the drive into the tablet computer sitting on the desk. She put the vodka on the table with a wet thunk. He nodded at the tablet screen and powered it down. "These are good?"

"They don't change," Zoya said, wiping at her nose with the back of her hand. "The Combine is far too powerful to care."

"Our plans might change their mind," Volk said and turned to her. She was ready for him, shoving the photo into his chest.

"My mother is sentimental," she said, watching him as he smoothed the photo between his fingers. "By the looks of your wall out there, that is something you both share. Maybe you'll want this for your collection."

He smiled, a slow turn of lips. For a second, she could see the boy in him, the soft curves hidden in hard edges, but then it vanished, and he handed it back to her.

"You'll want it for your journey, unless you join us," he said. "Some of us have been waiting for you."

She looked up at him, surprised. "For what? To be Viktor's daughter, the Nationalist mascot? I have no interest."

"The cause is interested," he said, and she snatched the photo from him.

"I'm not," Zoya said curtly, thinking of her mother where she'd left her. Guilt gnawed at her stomach, and she wanted desperately for it to be gone. Her Mama had left her when her father died, preferring a world that didn't exist in her drugs and hallucinations. It was a place Zoya could not follow, and her mother would refuse to follow Zoya.

This was the only way.

"Then keep it," he suggested as she folded the photo and slipped it into her pocket. "You'll want it more where you're going, and I don't need the memories."

Volk picked up the vodka and took Zoya's wrist, leading her into an alcove with a squat toilet behind a sheet of plywood and a cracked sink that trickled water. A trail of rust slipped down the drain.

"I have your papers," Volk said as he busied himself setting out a knife, a pad of gauze, surgical tape. "The train is leaving with a shipment tonight, so we must be quick."

He unscrewed the vodka and pressed it into her hands. She took two healthy gulps and gasped as she nodded her understanding. She pushed the vodka back at him and turned away, busying herself with the graffiti on the walls. Volk picked up the knife and held it over the open flame that lit the room with shivers of warm orange light.

"Lift your right wrist," he said, and Zoya found herself smiling.

The knife bit quick, blood pooling and trickling into the sink. Zoya forced herself to hold still, forced herself to breathe deep, and made herself turn to watch as Volk finally worked the chip free.

It fell into the sink, sticking to the porcelain. Volk

cleaned away the blood and doused the cut with vodka, wrenching another hiss out of Zoya.

"I'm not sorry," he said to her, pressing the gauze against the wound.

"Sadist," she murmured, looking down at her wrist wrapped in his long fingers.

"To the core," he smiled and put one hand on the crown of her head, looking at her with what she thought was a flash of affection.

"Alexei," she started, beginning to shift from him.

"You are free, Zoya Ivanova," he said, his fingers slipping out of her hair. "Now comes the hard part."

The train carried her to the river of ice, and the Skopa crashed through it with bone jarring ease. Zoya curled herself into an empty freight container in the bowels of the ship, her bag a poor excuse for a pillow and the provided bucket a longing reminder that Hamburg was two weeks away. The Skopa rocked back and forth, the sound of ice exploding against the hull keeping Zoya from sleep. The first mate attended to her in secret, squirreling away pieces of bread and cups of water, slipping them into her crate. When she was too tired to move during these visits, he would kneel down and stroke grease-stained fingers through her hair.

"Where are we?" she would ask above her water cup,

and he would only shake his head.

"The time goes faster if you do not know," he said and took away the empty tray, leaving her with a flashlight to cut through the dark.

Zoya turned the flashlight on as soon as the container door shut and locked her in, the fragile beam bouncing off the metal and lighting up her rectangle of space. She sat in the middle, dragging her bag into her lap, and ripped it open with shaking hands.

She'd packed so few things. Underwear, a toothbrush, socks, the papers Volk had fashioned. None of that was needed in the crate. Zoya upended the bag, scattering belongings, until she came to the packet of photos and dumped them into her lap.

The hard part, he had said. Hardly. Entrapment on the open ocean was nothing to her ignorance. She went through the photos, sorting them, leaving finger smears on printed faces, searched the backs for information that was nearly always there and written in her mother's hand. There was only one of Alexei, still sloppily folded in her back pocket, but many of her father. Viktor laughing, smiling, straight-faced, and stern. Only a few of her mother, the photographer, the keeper of the memories.

So many of Zoya. Zoya, aged 1. Zoya, aged 5. Zoya and Viktor.

There was a time, Zoya thought, when Mama loved

her, maybe fiercely. The guilt rose up. Zoya was afraid it would burrow into her heart. She pushed the photos together, tucking them back into the envelope, when a lone photo slipped free and fell into her lap.

A photo of a cabin, surrounded by trees. Zoya had never seen trees.

Гавань, her mother's neat handwriting said on the back. Haven.

And an address, words written in German that Zoya couldn't puzzle out on the Skopa.

She flopped over onto her back and turned off the flashlight, letting the container plunge into darkness. It was her fault. She could have asked. She could have stayed. She had been invited, offered the secrets kept underneath Mechanika, and she'd said no.

She'd only wanted to leave. Even now, she still wanted only to leave.

So she slept, paced, kept track of the time in cups of water.

It was when the container lifted and swung, scattering her things and sending her rolling into the side with a sickening thud, that Zoya knew it was time. They landed on solid ground, and she stood shakily to her feet. Gathered her things. Blinked her eyes wearily at the door when it cracked open. She peered at it from under a dirty curtain of hair.

The first mate smiled at her wide enough to reveal one broken tooth.

"Welcome to Hamburg."

The walk was long, but Zoya didn't mind it. The winter was crisp here, the air blue and sweet. The snow gathered in white fluff, glittering in an untouched carpet as she stamped through it. On the way to the house, Zoya stopped every few yards to cup the stuff in her hands simply to marvel at it.

The house could be glimpsed in the distance, a cottage set in a limitless stand of trees. The trees towered above her, quaking under ice. Zoya ran her bare fingers over the bark, stared up in wonder at plants that grew taller than houses. She could hardly feel the cold. It did not soak into her bones like before.

Zoya checked the address again from the back of the photo. Mama's writing seemed warm in her hand, and Zoya carefully slipped it back in her pocket before she walked up the slippery steps to the cottage door and knocked, not knowing what she would find inside.

Somewhere in the depths of the ice forest, a wolf howled. High and mournful, until others joined the call.

The door opened.

Mara Dabrishus grew up in the Arkansas Ozarks and currently resides in Northeast Ohio with her husband and two cats. Outside of writing, her favorite thing is riding horses in circles, loops, and perfect figure eights. Her debut novel, *Stay the Distance*, was released in early 2015.

MAVERICK

By Cathy Bryant

The teenage boy at the end of the corridor beckoned to us.

"Here! You'd best scarper! There's a bunch of 'em heading this way. Come with me. I know a way through."

By way of reply Jack sprayed him with plasm from the ghostgun, and the boy gave a thin howl as he disappeared.

"How did you know?" I asked.

"The word 'scarper,'" said Jack. "No one's used it since the 1970s. He was obviously an S-ghost out to lifesteal."

I shuddered. One touch and Super-Ghosts could possess your body and live the life left in it—and you'd be the bodiless phantasm, floating and wandering and not much else. You wouldn't even be an S-ghost after that, but a mere pale, powerless thing.

"You're amazing," I said to Jack. He was, too. He'd

killed more S-ghosts than anyone else, and it didn't hurt that he was also tall, strong and handsome.

"Thanks, Shelley," he said and tried to pat me on the head, which was annoying. I ducked away from his touch.

"I'm not a kid. I'm thirteen," I muttered, and he held his hands up, palms out, in apology.

Soon we made our way back to the centre. It was getting bigger day by day as more human refugees—other survivors of the First Ghost War—found us, and as people fought their way outwards, securing more territory.

It was a dynamic military operation, apart from Jack's actions, that is. He couldn't take orders and couldn't be patient and methodical, but as a maverick loner he was tolerated because of his massive hit rate. It was largely thanks to him that the S-ghosts were starting to recede.

He taught me so many things, especially ways to spot the enemy. Jack could always tell a human from a ghost by the smell and when their mouths watered hungrily.

"That's another giveaway," explained Jack. "Look for appetite in the eyes and salivating or swallowing."

"I've learned so much from you," I said softly to Jack at the end of my training period. "You'll never know how grateful I am."

I grasped his hand in mine and sucked him right out of his body. Oh, it felt good, felt strong to have muscles, to have legs, to breathe.

Jack made his last human sound, a scream that suddenly cut off as he became a standard powerless ghost, with no hope of getting a body back. He drifted away, helpless to do anything at all.

I ran west of the centre, using Jack's easy lope. I was sure to find more S-ghosts on the road, to whom I could pass on all the things that had given our dead comrades away. My knowledge would gain us thousands of lives, and we would finally beat the vicious humans.

They might call me a maverick back at the ghost camp, but they can't argue with my results.

Cathy Bryant worked as a life model, civil servant and childminder before becoming a professional writer. She has won fourteen literary awards, including the Bulwer-Lytton Fiction Prize, and her work has appeared in over 200 publications including *The Huffington Post*. Cathy has had two poetry collections published by small presses, and Cathy's latest book is the Jane Austen-themed murder mystery novel *Pride and Regicide*, published by Crooked Cat. See more at www.cathybryant.co.uk, and see Cathy's monthly listings for financially-challenged writers at www.compsandcalls.com. She lives in Cheshire, UK.

WHERE THE DEATH STORMS BLOW

Hope Erica Schultz

Happy Birthday to me," Erin muttered, drying the last dish. Her reflection looked back at her from the metal serving platter, gray eyes unblinking, short brown curls disarrayed, mouth twisted into a self-pitying grimace. She resisted the urge to stick out her tongue and handed the dish off to her brother.

Karl smiled crookedly as he stowed the platter on the top shelf she couldn't reach. "Gram said you could have your cake tonight."

Erin shook her head. "I'll wait for Mom and Dad. It's just that it's another year before I can do anything. I should be out with them, or monitoring, like Gram. Anyone can babysit."

213

"You're in charge," her brother reproved. "That's important, too." His eyes were brown, like their father's, but otherwise it was like looking at her reflection. Her taller, male reflection.

Erin looked over into the dining room where her seven cousins were busy playing a game of charades around the enormous oak table. Carrie was acting out something that had the others laughing uncontrollably, unable to guess any more. Last year she would have joined in. A year ago she hadn't realized how desperately important the work was, so important that all four of Gram's children, with their kids and spouses, had relocated to a secret underground bunker on a mountain in the middle of nowhere.

The world had been ending since before she was born. The only difference was that she understood it now.

Erin shook her head at the thoughts and retreated from the others into the false front room, a rustic cabin that could have belonged in nearly any time or place. Karl followed and closed the secret door behind them, cutting off the sound of laughter. The door disappeared into the wall around it, masking the entrance to the bunker from the cabin. Fading winter light from the windows lit the room in shades of purple gray.

Erin knelt by the fireplace with the snoring greyhounds; Sheba opened one eye and thumped her brindle tail, while slate gray Lance whined in his sleep. She scratched Sheba's head absently, staring at the fire.

"You'll be sixteen over a year before I am," Karl pointed out.

Erin nodded glumly. "I know. I wouldn't mind so much if they didn't need me, need somebody to help. Without Gram, nobody would even know about the dogs or how to survive a shift outside. We're doing more research here than the rest of the world combined . . . and there are only nine people doing it. Ten, in a year, if they actually let me help. Mom said I could start at sixteen, but Dad . . .."

Karl nodded. They both knew how protective their father could be.

The greyhounds twitched, lifting their heads from the braided rug. The alarm sounded a heartbeat later, a thrumming that cut through the silence. Beneath it, Erin could feel a vibration in her bones.

"We're shifting? Now?" Karl started. "Mom and Dad are out there!"

Erin stood and lit candles hurriedly as the world went dark outside the window. There were colors in the blackness, colors that didn't exist—and shouldn't. "Gram will get them home. Is there anything high tech out here?"

Karl picked up a book by the fire, a doll by the front door, and disappeared into the back. She heard voices rise to question him, then the door being closed and bolted from inside as he returned.

"Alex will take the little ones below," he reported. "Carrie will watch the door in case we need her."

The front room was a convincing log cabin, built against the hillside; candle light turned the walls to gold. It would look normal enough in any world that had developed the ability to work iron. It was their disguise, their way of semi-safely interacting with whatever world they shifted to.

Outside the shifting realities settled to one. The strange colors bled back into darkness, and the darkness paled to a winter afternoon. The worlds had stopped colliding.

Sheba began to growl, then stood and paced to the door. Lance pushed by her, tail wagging. Erin hesitated, then threw on her coat and boots. Plain and handmade, like everything in this part of the house they should pass as normal if they encountered strangers.

"Do you think it's them?" Karl asked. He grabbed his outdoor clothing and handed her a wool hat and mittens.

"Probably not; Gram will need time to guide them back. But if it's them, we can help." Erin snapped leashes onto the dogs' collars and opened the door; Sheba lunged forward as Karl took Lance's leash. Karl pulled the front door shut as they headed out into the twilight.

The snow was falling, accumulating in small drifts among the trees.

"Beats chores," Karl quipped; Erin smiled and walked

faster. The mountain was similar to the one they usually lived on, but the trees were different.

Erin let Sheba guide her, trusting the dogs through the fading light. She thought they'd gone a quarter mile, maybe more, when Sheba growled and Lance whined. Through the snow she could see someone huddled against a tree. It was too small to be anyone from her parents' research team. Erin hesitated, then stepped forward.

In the fading light she saw a boy, Karl's age, holding a bundle of rags. He was dressed in coarse homespun—either very poor, or this was a primitive world—and even in the darkness she could see his thinness. Erin felt her breath catch as the bundle in his arms moved; it was a baby.

The boy met her eyes. "We need shelter. I've a knife, to trade."

"Erin—" Karl warned, but she ignored her brother, reaching out a hand to help the boy up. His hands were bare, and he shivered as he met her eyes.

"Come with us," she said firmly. The boy held the baby in his arms; he staggered, walking, and Erin resisted the urge to help him. The hills were barren as far as she could see, with no hope of shelter for this pair of wanderers . . . or for her parents, who were likely out in it.

There really was no choice. Erin bit her lip, then turned Sheba towards home. "The baby," she began.

"My sister," the boy corrected.

"Your sister," Erin agreed. "When did she last eat?"

"Yesterday."

Erin winced. "We'll find her some milk."

"Erin!" Karl hissed again, and she turned to glower at him.

"Do you have a better idea? I don't see a convenient farm, let alone a motel, do you?"

Karl opened his mouth to argue, then they both froze as Sheba stopped, her ears up and listening.

Erin swore under her breath. "Grab hold!" She grasped the boy's arm with her free hand. Karl held his greyhound, the boy tried to pull away, and then the world moved beneath them.

It was worse, rawer out here. In the gathering dark Erin could see hills and trees altering, and she felt the thrumming in her teeth.

"Close your eyes!" she yelled; her voice sounded alien and harsh, like the shift. Sheba pulled forward, and she followed, still dragging the boy. A dozen feet in shifting realities, a hundred—and then Sheba pulled sharply sideways, and the cabin was in front of them, windows bright.

"Erin, the rules," Karl hissed.

She shook her head.

"They'll never get home!" he persisted.

Erin hesitated a moment, then pulled the pair to the

doorway. "They'd die," she replied softly. "I don't think cultural contamination matters, next to that."

"Dad is going to freak," Karl muttered, but she ignored him as she led them inside. In the firelight the boy's clothing and rough shoes were as primitive as she'd thought, but she was startled just a bit to see that his hair was blond.

"It was a Death Storm," the boy said, shaking. "Nothing survives a Death Storm."

"Nothing except Greyhounds," Karl muttered. Erin kicked him as she pulled the pair in front of the fire. The boy didn't resist as she pulled off his coat and shoes; his feet were dangerously pale. The infant—likely closer to a toddler, but far too thin—was unresponsive, her neck as cold as the boy's feet when Erin knelt to touch her.

Erin took a deep breath. "We need to take them into the back." Karl began to protest, and she cut him off. "If not, he's going to lose his feet, and we'll lose the baby altogether. I need hot water, and now—not when the fire can warm it."

Karl looked at the dirty baby, at the boy staring uncomprehendingly. "I could call Gram on the radio."

Erin shook her head. "With two shifts in fifteen minutes, she can't spare a moment. It's my call."

She focused on the boy as Karl did what she'd asked. He wouldn't release the child, so she led them both to the secret door, the false room behind, and the living area beyond. The boy blinked, too dazed to question electric lights, the bathing room, or even the great tub that could hold six of her cousins. Carrie had the water running, as Karl warmed milk for the baby.

She shed her coat and boots beside the tub and led them into it. The water was warm, and the boy flinched slightly. The little one stirred, then began to cry.

"Why are we alive?" the boy asked, cradling the baby in his arms, his eyes almost closing in the warmth. "That was a Death Storm."

"Greyhounds—the kind of dog we have—can find their way through the storms. It's something special about them, connected to their blood." Erin bit her lip, trying to think how to explain the electromagnetic effects of high hemo-globin counts, and then shook her head. "What matters is that you're safe now." The boy looked nearly asleep and she turned her attention to the baby, checking her feet for frostbite. As Erin unwrapped the rags from the little girl's hands, the boy jerked awake, pulling the child away.

"I won't let you hurt her," he said, a crude knife suddenly in one hand, blue eyes wide and desperate.

Erin saw Carrie and Karl start forward; she held her hands up soothingly. "Why would we hurt her?" she asked softly.

"Don't pretend she'll pass her Naming Day," he retorted. "They'll kill her, because of her hands."

The child stared, unblinking; her small hand held six perfect fingers. Erin's fists clenched—kill for a harmless mutation? "They won't kill her," she promised. "They'll never find her."

She looked the boy in the eye, understanding what she was promising. Karl was right, Dad would freak, but that didn't matter. There were more important things than rules.

"They'll never find her," she repeated. "You're ours now."

Hope Erica Schultz lives in Central Massachusetts with her spouse, two children, one dog, four cats, and assorted visiting wildlife. She writes SF and fantasy stories and novels that can be considered comedy, adventure, or horror depending on where she chooses to end them. When not writing, reading, or pretending to be someone else, she still works for a living. Find her on Facebook at facebook.com/hope.schultz.14